D0053024

DATE DUE

AG 13 '05	
JE 01 '06	
SE 17 '07	
JE 25 '09	
SE 16 '11	
MR 07 '19	

Demco, Inc. 38-294

DEC 10 '96
JAN 13 '97
APR 3 '97
MAY 21 '97
JUN 2 '97
JUL 8 '97
AUG 14 '97
SEP 8 '97
JUN 16 '98
SE 24 '98
MY 21 '99
FE 24 01
NO 6 '01

DO

D

M

LO

BANT

NEW YORK • TORONTO

COLOMA PUBLIC LIBRARY

RL5.6, age 012 and up

Don't Die, My Love
A Bantam Book / August 1995

The Starfire logo is a registered trademark of Bantam Books,
a division of Bantam Doubleday Dell Publishing Group, Inc.
Registered in U.S. Patent and Trademark Office and elsewhere.

All rights reserved.
Text Copyright © 1995 by Lurlene McDaniel
Cover art copyright © 1995 by Jim Galante

ISBN 0-553-56715-2

CHAPTER SAMPLER ISBN: 0-553-57081-1

Bantam Books are published by Bantam Books, a division of Bantam
Doubleday Dell Publishing Group, Inc. Its trademark, consisting of
the words "Bantam Books" and the portrayal of a rooster, is
Registered in U.S. Patent and Trademark Office and in other
countries. Marca Registrada. Bantam Books, 1540 Broadway, New
York, New York 10036.

PRINTED IN THE UNITED STATES OF AMERICA

Dr. Portage sat and steepled his fingers together. "I've checked Luke over, listened to his symptoms, and done some preliminary blood work. As I told you on the phone, I'm concerned about his elevated white blood count."

Julie felt her heart pounding and reached for Luke's hand. "Luke, he's scaring me."

Luke looked away. His hand felt cold as ice.

"I don't mean to alarm any of you," Dr. Portage said. "But I don't like what I'm seeing. I suspect Luke has some kind of infection. According to his records, he's been treated with antibiotics, but he hasn't responded as he should have."

"Are you saying you'll have to run more tests?" Nancy asked.

"Yes. And he needs to be in the hospital in order to run them. I've got a call in to St. Paul's Hospital in Chicago."

"Why Chicago? What's wrong with Waterton General?"

"They don't have the equipment and staff I want for Luke."

Julie and Luke exchanged glances. His dark eyes bored into her, making her even more afraid. "What do you mean?" Julie asked. Her voice quivered.

Dr. Portage looked directly at Luke. "I want you to go home, pack a bag, and drive straight to St. Paul's."

VOID

1

"I'll get the door!" Julie Ellis called, bounding down the stairs from her bedroom. She yanked open the heavy front door to see Luke Muldenhower on her front porch. He grinned as she pulled open the glass storm door and threw herself into his arms. "I've missed you," she cried, snuggling against his chest.

"Blame your father," he said, kissing her. "He's the one who made the team stay for the championship game. It wasn't fun watching the finals, feeling like it should have been us playing for the state title."

Indiana's Waterton Warriors football team, whom Julie's father coached, had made it all the way to the state football finals in their division. On Thursday, the school had shut down. Buses were chartered and most of the town had taken the trip to Indianapolis for the playoffs. Waterton had lost in the semifinals, and while the students and fans, including Julie and her mother, had returned glum and deflated, the players had remained behind until Saturday night to watch the game for first place.

Her father had returned only hours before. And Julie had been waiting anxiously for Luke to drop his stuff at his house, then come see her. She was sorry they'd lost, not only for the sake of school pride, but because she knew how much winning meant to both Luke and her father.

She led him into the living room, where a fire crackled in the fireplace, warding off the late-November chill, and sat him down beside her on the sofa. "Believe me, Mom and I've heard every detail about how bad things went for us. If only time hadn't run out . . . If only Bobby Spencer had hit his man in the end zone with ten seconds left on the clock in the third quarter . . . If only the referee hadn't called a holding penalty on the final play . . ." Julie ticked off the reasons she knew by heart. "Dad's been over every minute of that game and why we lost it."

She gave Luke a pouty look. "But enough

about the game. This is our first date in months that doesn't revolve around football, and I don't want to talk about anything except us and how wonderful you think I am."

He laughed and hugged her. "You're wonderful."

"And?"

"And I love you like crazy." He pressed his forehead against hers and kissed the tip of her turned-up nose.

"That's better," she said with a sly smile. "Forget about football tonight. Next year, *you'll* be the senior quarterback, and you'll take us to the state finals. For now, the season's over. Let's talk about the Christmas dance. It's only three weeks away. Do we want to double with Solena and Frank? You know how they're always fighting with each other."

Luke didn't have a chance to answer, because Bud Ellis, Julie's father, walked into the living room. "I thought I heard you come in," the coach said.

Instantly, Luke was on his feet, his hand outstretched. "Hey, Coach. Sorry about the game."

"Not your fault," Bud Ellis insisted. "I should never have pulled you out and put

Spencer in. You were doing great, but you looked tired."

"It's this flu. I'm having trouble shaking it."

"You look like you feel all right now," Coach said, his gaze flitting between Luke and Julie's radiant face.

"Julie's good medicine," Luke said, taking hold of her hand and pulling her up alongside him.

"We've got a date," Julie told her father. "No more football season. No more curfews."

"*You* have a curfew," her father reminded her.

"Curfew, shmurfew." Julie put her hands on her hips. "Tonight we're going bowling and then we're going to eat a goopy, gooey hot fudge sundae, and since tomorrow's Sunday, Luke can sleep in 'til noon before he has to come take me out to the mall."

"Hot fudge sundaes! Sleeping 'til noon!" Her father looked horrified. "Don't go spoiling my prize quarterback and making him soft, Julie-girl."

Julie knew that would be impossible. Luke had a muscular physique to die for, made harder by the playing season plus hours of daily weight training in the gym. "The only soft thing about Luke is *me*," she said with a flounce of her blond hair. "And whose side are you on anyway? *I'm* your flesh and blood."

Her father grinned and chucked her under the chin. "Yeah, but you can't play football. And you throw like a girl."

She knew her dad was teasing, but still his remark stung. She was her parents' only child. And a daughter at that. She had never doubted that her dad loved her, but Luke was clearly the son Bud Ellis had always wished he had.

Luke reached his arm around her waist and pulled her next to him. "And I, for one, wouldn't want it any other way. Julie's just about perfect, I'd say."

She felt gratitude for his gentle defense of her. "We're supposed to meet Solena and Frank at the bowling alley in fifteen minutes," Julie said, glancing at the antique clock on the fireplace mantel.

Luke helped her with her coat, and they'd gotten as far as the front door before her father said, "Some college coaches are sniffing around about you already, Luke."

Luke stopped and turned. "They are? Who?"

Inwardly, Julie groaned. It was unfair of her father to hold out this carrot when he knew they were in a hurry. "Can't you talk to Luke tomorrow about this?"

"I could," her dad said.

But Luke wasn't budging. "Tell me, Coach . . . Who's asking?"

"Ohio State for one."

"No lie?" Luke broke into a grin. "One of the Big Ten's asking about me?"

"You're good, Luke; they *should* be asking. And you've still got another year in high school. They'll be on you like white on rice after next season."

Julie refrained from rushing the discussion even though they were going to be impossibly late. Football was Luke's *only* chance to make it into college.

"So what did you tell him?" Luke asked.

"I told him to stand in line!"

Both Luke and her father burst out laughing. Julie smiled and shook her head. "You two are totally weird." But she was glad for Luke. She loved him and wanted him to receive every break he deserved.

Once outside in the crisp November night, Luke took her in his arms and kissed her long and hard. She felt her knees go weak. "I guess you really *did* miss me," she whispered when he released her.

"Now that the season's over, I've got to make up for lost time. You know I love you, Julie."

"I know. But it's always nice to hear you say it."

He opened the door of his car for her. The vehicle was old, but clean and well maintained. Luke had worked long hours the summer before to earn the money to buy it, and when he'd turned seventeen in October, his mom, who worked at the steel mills, had gotten it painted a deep navy blue. The car caught the color of the pale full moon in its shiny finish.

They drove to Waterton's lone bowling alley, parked, and went inside. The sounds of balls striking pins punctuated the air. Frank sauntered over. "Sorry we're late," Luke said. "Where's Solena?"

"In the bathroom sulking."

"Don't tell me you two have had another fight," Julie said in exasperation.

"She's impossible, Julie. Why's she so jealous?"

Julie shot Luke a look that said, *Let me go see what I can do,* and headed for the rest rooms. She found Solena inside, dabbing her eyes with a paper towel. "Now what's wrong?"

Julie asked, none too patiently. She'd been looking forward to an evening of fun, not of refereeing her friends' spats.

"I caught Frank talking to Melanie Hawkins."

"It's not a federal offense."

Solena threw down the wadded towel. "It might not seem like any big deal to you— you've got Luke, who's never even so much as looked at another girl since he fell for you in fifth grade. But out here in the *real* world, it's pretty grim. Girls are always coming on to Frank. And he likes it!"

"Frank likes you, Solena. How many times do I have to tell you? And I know girls are waiting to snake away guys like Frank and Luke, but give your guy some credit. If he wants to date Melanie, he'll tell you."

"Oh, you just don't understand!" Solena stamped her foot.

Julie was trying to be sympathetic, but it was difficult. It was true that Luke had hung around her since he was ten. Of course, then, she couldn't see him for dust. In fact, she'd found it annoying to have some skinny, scrappy kid with shaggy black hair following her everywhere. But when he was twelve, he joined one of the football teams sponsored by the YMCA that her father coached and she learned more about him.

She learned that Luke's father had died in a steel mill accident when Luke was only eight and that his mother was struggling to raise him alone. She learned that he was always in trouble and solving his problems with his fists. Football and her father's belief in Luke as a player had saved him from growing up in the juvenile detention center.

On her fourteenth birthday, Luke had shown up on Julie's porch holding a fistful of flowers, and when she'd taken them and looked into his dark brown eyes and seen absolute adoration for her, something inside her had melted. They'd been dating steadily for the past three years and everyone knew that Julie and Luke went together like ice cream and cake, sunlight and summer.

"We're going bowling," Julie told Solena firmly. "And if you don't join us, Melanie really *will* have an opening. Is that what you want?"

Once she'd coaxed Solena out of the bathroom and they'd found Luke and Frank setting up in one of the lanes, Julie felt better. Solena sulked for a while longer, but soon she seemed like her old self. Julie sat nestled against Luke's side while Solena and Frank took their turn at the pins.

"Glad you could soften her up," Luke said, tugging playfully on Julie's blond hair.

"I wasn't about to let Solena ruin our evening. Besides, I have plans for you later, buster." She pressed her lips against his neck.

"What plans?" he asked, a smile in his voice.

She pulled back, looking puzzled. She reached up and pressed her fingers along the side of his jaw. "Luke," she said. "What's this lump?"

2

Luke pulled away, his expression self-conscious. "Swollen gland, that's all."

"Did your doctor see it?"

"Julie, it's nothing. When a person gets the flu, glands swell."

She frowned. "Is the one on the other side swollen too?"

Luke stood and picked up his bowling ball. "Are you going to hang out your shingle?" He held up an imaginary sign. " 'Julie Ellis: Medicine Woman.' Come on, it's our turn. Bet you a buck you can't make a strike."

She leaped to her feet. "You're on, buster."

The rest of the evening passed quickly, and by the time Luke drove her home, Julie was feeling content. She hooked her arm through Luke's once he stopped his car in front of her house, then leaned her head against his broad shoulder. "I had fun," she said.

"Me too. But then I always have fun when I'm with you."

She felt a tingling sensation along her skin. Luke said romantic things without calculation. Which was one of the reasons she cared for him so much. "I think you should sleep in tomorrow," she told him. "You need a chance to recuperate."

He didn't argue. "I am feeling pretty lousy. Maybe some extra sleep will help. I'll call you after you get home from church."

She raised her face and received his long, lingering kiss, then got out of the car. "I can make it up the walk by myself. Go home and get to bed."

He smiled, but even in the faint glow of the lights from his dashboard, she thought he looked weary and pale. She squeezed his hand through the open passenger window and dashed up the sidewalk and into her house.

"Is that you, Julie?" she heard her mother call.

"No, Mom. It's a burglar."

Her mother came into the foyer, her terry-cloth robe wrapped around her slim figure.

"Cute," she said, without humor. "Come sit down and visit with me."

"I'm tired. Can we talk tomorrow?" Julie was certain she knew what her mother was going to say, and she wasn't in the mood to hear it. Especially after the good time she'd had with Luke and her friends.

"You'll be too busy tomorrow." Her mother led her into the living room, sat, and patted the sofa cushion beside her. "Come on. It won't take long."

Julie sighed and scrunched herself into the corner of the plush rose-colored sofa. She hugged a throw pillow to her chest. "So, what can't wait until tomorrow?"

"Julie, I'm concerned that you're not sending out applications for college."

"Oh, Mom—not this again." Julie groaned.

"Listen to me. I'm a guidance counselor, for heaven's sake. I know what I'm talking about. The freshman classes for all the really top colleges fill up fast and you're too bright, your grades are too good, for you not to get into any college you apply to. I've already talked to dozens of kids in your junior class, and they're sending off forms right and left. You should be too."

"Mom, I've got tons of time to think about

college. I won't even take the SAT exam until next fall, and those scores are what colleges really consider."

"Naturally the SATs are important, but you won't have any trouble with them. You should start applying now to the colleges you're truly interested in."

Julie struggled to keep from losing her temper. She knew her mother was trying to be helpful, but all Julie felt was unnecessary pressure. "Can't I just enjoy high school? Good grief, it's not even Christmas yet! I don't want to deal with college now—especially when I have over a year of high school left." She got up from the sofa.

"It's because of Luke, isn't it?" Her mother's voice was low, but it stopped Julie in her tracks.

"I don't know what you mean."

"You're so busy thinking about Luke that you don't think about yourself. You spend more time with him than with anything else."

Julie clenched her teeth, hating that her mother was partly right, yet not wanting to admit it. "Of course I like Luke. But I do plenty of things with my friends. And I've never once let my grades drop, have I?"

"Julie, I'm not trying to be a nag. It's just that I want so much more for you."

Julie spun and peered down at her mother on the sofa. "More of *what?* Why shouldn't I have a boyfriend and have fun with him? What have you got against Luke?"

"I haven't got anything against him. He's a nice boy. But I want to see you go to college. I want you to get out of this smelly little steel town. Have a career. See the world."

Julie rolled her eyes. *The same old argument.* "Mom, just because you hate Waterton doesn't mean I do. Daddy and I both love it here." By bringing her father into the discussion, Julie felt a sense of leverage. It was true that her dad liked the small steel town where he'd grown up and where he now held the job of athletic director and football coach for northwest Indiana's top-rated high school.

"And don't forget," she added hastily, before her mother could react. "Luke's going to get a football scholarship and be out of here in two years. So, based on your logic, why would I even want to stay if he's gone?"

Her mother's hands, folded in her lap, appeared rigid, as if she were gripping something so tightly that she couldn't let go. "I wasn't badgering you, Julie. I only want you to think about *your* future. Not Luke's."

"I do think about my future. I'll go to college, Mom. And I won't end up at any 'Podunk University,' either." She bent and kissed her mother quickly on the forehead. "Now, I've got to get to bed. It's late and I promised Mrs. Poston I'd help her with Sunday school class in the morning."

Julie breezed from the room and up the stairs without giving her mother a chance to stop her. And once safely in her room, she flopped on the bed and exhaled deeply. She'd heard her father say many times, *The best offense is a good defense.* And that was what she'd offered her mother tonight—a great defense.

Julie wasn't fibbing when she'd said she wanted to go away to college. But what she hadn't said was that she wasn't about to choose a college until she knew where Luke was going to attend. Hadn't her father said that college coaches were already lining up to offer Luke athletic scholarships? Well, once Luke got down to serious negotiations, Julie would begin to apply to those colleges.

She knew her mother wouldn't like her plans, but right now, Julie didn't care. She wasn't about to spend four years apart from Luke Muldenhower. Besides, her mother was right about one thing: Julie Ellis was smart, and as long as she kept her grades up, she figured she could get into most any college she wanted.

And Solena was right about something too: the world was full of girls waiting to steal a guy like Luke. "I won't let that happen," Julie said out loud. "Not in a million years."

She loved Luke with all her heart. And she wasn't about to let him get away.

"I think you have a fever, Luke." Julie pressed her hand on his cheek as she spoke. Automatically, she moved her hand to the side of his neck, to where she'd first felt the swollen gland the night before. "And your gland doesn't seem any smaller."

It was Sunday afternoon and he'd come over to study with her. Their books were strewn across the dining room table, but Luke had spent most of the past hour resting his head on the book in front of him.

"I'm fine," he said, not too kindly. "You're not my mother, Julie—get off my case."

"Well, excuse me for being concerned." Julie shoved her chair backward and stood up.

"Wait a minute. I didn't mean to snap at you. I didn't sleep good last night, and today I've got a pounding headache."

Instantly, she was sorry for being cross with him. "Why don't you go back to your doctor?"

He shrugged. "I just don't want to. What's he going to do? Give me another prescription for antibiotics? The last prescription didn't help."

"Then that's all the more reason to go."

Pale November sun shone through the window and shimmered in waves across the table. "Office visits and prescriptions cost money," he said. "Things are tight with Mom this month. She doesn't need any extra expense."

Julie knew it was hard for Luke to talk to her about his poverty. Ever since his father's death, his mother had worked full-time and he had worked summer jobs, but there still never seemed to be enough money to go around. "She has health insurance from her job at the mill," Julie said. "She'll get reimbursed."

"Yeah, but she has to pay up front, then wait for the insurance company to reimburse her."

"So what's your point?" Julie crossed her arms, refusing to back down.

Luke tossed his pencil on the table. "My point is that I don't want Mom to spend the money for some stupid flu bug that will eventually run its course."

"That is *so* dumb, Luke Muldenhower. Tell my dad and he'll see to it that you get to the doctor. And it won't cost you a thing!"

He shoved away from the table and stood. "I don't need charity, Julie. It's my flu, you know. And I don't want your daddy to foot my bills."

"That's the *dumbest—*"

She got no further. Luke stepped around her and headed out the door. She called for him to return, but all she heard was the slamming of the front door behind him.

3

"What's all the noise about?" Julie's father sauntered into the dining room, part of the Sunday paper in his hand, his reading glasses pushed down his nose.

"Nothing," Julie said. Suddenly, she realized she sounded just like Luke, saying things were fine when they weren't. "We had a little disagreement and Luke left."

"He'll come back when he's cooled off," her father said. "But don't be hard on my man, Julie-girl. Luke's had a rough season. He doesn't need hassle from his girl."

"Well, thank you, Dad, for your support. Did it occur to you that Luke might be the one in the wrong in this?"

Her father threw up his hands, the paper dangling limply. "Hold on. I'm not about to get in the middle of some lovers' spat. I was just wondering why the door slammed so hard."

Julie thought it ironic that her father could be so high on her relationship with Luke and her mother so down on it. Traditionally, such things tended to be the other way around, but her father had always had a soft spot for Luke and Julie had often felt that he'd take Luke's side against anyone—including his own daughter. "Next time Luke leaves in a huff, I'll tell him not to slam the door," she said.

He started to say something, but the phone rang and her mother called, "Bud, it's for you."

"Back in a minute," he said to Julie. "And we'll discuss what set Luke off."

Julie didn't want any discussion. If Luke wanted her father to know how bad he was feeling, he'd have to tell him. She wasn't about to after the way he'd carried on over a measly doctor's visit.

Twenty minutes later, her father was still on the phone when the doorbell sounded.

Luke was standing on the porch, looking contrite, his hands behind his back. "Can I come in?"

Julie pushed open the door, turned on her

heel, and headed to the dining room, with Luke tagging after her.

"Here. These are for you." He held out a small bouquet of flowers. She recognized them as the kind sold down at the Kroger grocery store, yet they conjured up memories of bouquets from the past he'd given her. It was his favorite means of communication.

"Do you think you can solve every problem with flowers?" She took them and buried her nose in the petals of the yellow and red mums.

"Can't I?"

He looked so cute and apologetic, she had a hard time not smiling. "Yes," she admitted. "You know how I feel about flowers."

He grinned. "And me? How do you feel about me? Am I forgiven?"

"I wasn't trying to tell you what to do," she said, returning to the topic of their disagreement. "I'm worried, that's all. You've been sick for weeks and you don't seem to be getting any better. I guess I can't understand why you don't go back to the doctor and demand he make you well. The football playoffs are over with now, so you really should go to the doctor. And money's no excuse."

He had sat down in a dining room chair while she talked. His long, lanky body drooped, reminding her of a balloon that was losing air. She thought he looked thinner than usual, but she wasn't about to mention it to him. "I know you're right," he said quietly. "I've been putting it off because . . . because I'm worried too."

"You are?"

"Other glands are swollen—the ones under my arms. And at night I get these terrible sweats. I mean I wake up and the sheets are soaking wet. I've been changing them every morning so Mom won't know."

Julie felt her stomach constrict. "This doesn't sound right to me. Maybe it's more than the flu."

"I guess I thought it would eventually go away."

"But it hasn't."

He shrugged. "Look, I'll go back to the doctor, but not until Christmas break."

"That's another three weeks!"

"I'm drowning in schoolwork. What with the playoffs and all, I really fell behind."

"But—"

He placed his fingertips across her lips to silence her. "Julie, I'm not smart like you. I have to work hard for my grades, and I can't slip up. Football scholarships to the best colleges mean you have to be a good athlete *and* a good student. The better my grades, the better my chances."

"But you have a whole year before you have to choose a college. Why not concentrate on your health now and work on your grades later?"

He shook his head and flashed a winsome smile. "Maybe you should be a lawyer. You're worse than a bulldog when you get hold of something. You just won't let it go, will you."

She felt her cheeks color. "I'm worried about you. Don't go brushing me off."

He got to his feet and wrapped his arms around her. She started to tug away, but his arms were strong and made her feel warm and safe. In his arms it didn't seem like anything was overly important, or frightening. "Besides," he said, "I've got to take my girl to a big formal dance. What if the doctor puts me on bed rest or something? How will I take her to the dance then?"

"I don't care if we miss the dance." Julie said the words, but knew it wasn't true. She really did want to go to the dance. She'd already bought her dress.

"Well, I care," Luke insisted. "It gives me another excuse to bring you flowers."

She pulled back and stared up into his face—the face she'd grown to love so much. "But the minute Christmas break starts, you'll go to the doctor?"

"Yes."

"Promise?"

"Unless I'm well, of course." He kissed the tip of her nose. "But you'll have to go with me. I really don't want to bother my mom with this. Not with Christmas and everything."

"You bet I'll go with you," Julie said. "In fact, I'll drive you personally."

He bent his head to kiss her mouth, but just then Coach Ellis came through the dining room doorway. Luke let Julie go. "Guess who I've been on the phone with," Coach said, looking excited. He didn't wait for their guesses. "The head of the school board. It looks as if those funds are going to be allocated for Waterton High to build that new football stadium."

Luke gave a high five. "All right!"

Julie knew how important the project was to her father. He'd been trying to push it through for over three years, but had met with steady setbacks. The present stadium was inadequate, since the number of kids attending the high school had grown so large. The often overflow crowd had to be accommodated on makeshift benches along the sidelines and the present bleachers were rickety, even hazardous. "That's great, Dad."

"I guess our being runner-up in the state made an impression on the board," Coach Ellis said, rubbing his hands together gleefully. "I'm going to get a jump start on this. I'll have an architect draw up some blueprints and be ready to lay them out for the board at their meeting in January."

"A new stadium." Luke's brown eyes gleamed. "When will it be finished?"

"If all goes according to my timetable, you could start your senior season in it."

Luke looked surprised. "That's not even a year from now."

"If it gets hustled through, we could break ground this spring. But it's not the construction that takes so long, it's getting the turf ready for play. It's possible that it could be ready by fall."

Luke shrugged. "Even if I can't play on it, the next class will. I'm just glad we're getting it."

"I want you to play on it." Coach Ellis sounded so adamant that Julie half believed he could have the grass grow on a schedule that met his demands.

Once he'd left the room, Julie turned toward Luke. "Dad sure doesn't let much get in the way of his goals for his football team, does he?"

"He's a great coach, Julie."

"He's the only coach you've ever had."

"No matter. He's a great coach by any standard. He doesn't teach you what to think out on the field; he teaches you *how* to think. I've learned everything I know about the game from him, and it's going to be my key for getting into college. And who knows—maybe even someday, the pros."

Julie felt a twinge of jealousy over the prominent place football held in Luke's life. Sometimes it seemed that the game was more the center of his world than she was. The feelings were childish, but that didn't stop them from coming. She wished she was as focused on something as Luke was on the sport of football. Maybe someday she would be, but right now, there was only Luke. "Well, if you go to the pros, I'll take out a franchise on you. How's that sound?"

"If I go to the pros, you're coming with me."

"Really? And what will I do? Organize your social calendar and commercial endorsements?"

"Not to worry—I'll find something for you to do." He plucked up one of the bright golden mums from the bouquet lying on the table and poked the stem through the silky blond hair above her ear. "I'll cover you in flowers someday, Julie-girl. And you won't be able to refuse me anything."

She laughed. "For every flower, you'll get a kiss."

"Promise?"

"Promise."

4

"**Y**our dress is awesome, Julie, and it really looks *great* on you." Solena was stretched across Julie's bed while Julie modeled for her. The dress's full taffeta skirt made a swishing sound as she pivoted toward the full-length mirror mounted on the back of her bedroom door.

She admired her reflection and the way the black fabric shimmered in the pale winter light coming through the windows. "You don't think it's too plain?"

"No way. It's elegant. And I love the way it falls off your shoulders. Pretty sexy."

The bodice fit perfectly and the neckline scooped downward and out to expose her creamy white shoulders and the swell of her breasts. "It cost me every penny of my Christmas gift money, plus a month's worth of baby-sitting funds, but I just fell in love with it. I had to have it."

"Wait 'til Luke sees it. He'll positively drool."

Julie smiled, imagining the look in his eyes when he saw her in the dress. "I like your dress too," she said, catching her friend's gaze in the mirror. "The color's perfect with your dark hair." They had come from Solena's house, where Solena had shown off her new dress.

"Next to you, I'll look like a frump tomorrow night."

"That's not true!"

Solena waved aside Julie's protest. "I can live with it. Just so long as I look better than Melanie."

"Are you still worried about her and Frank?"

"Maybe not worried . . . but I do want to be prepared." Solena scooted off the bed. "Let's run up to the mall and look for a new perfume. Frank needs an excuse to nuzzle my neck, don't you think?"

"I'd love to, but I can't. Luke's mom invited me for supper tonight."

"But it's only one o'clock. Supper's hours from now."

Julie didn't want to tell Solena the whole

truth, but this was the afternoon Luke was supposed to go to his doctor for another checkup. School had been out for a few days, but it had taken until today to get an appointment with the doctor. Half the town was down with the flu and Luke's doctor had been booked solid. "I promised him I'd come early," Julie told her friend.

"I'd say this qualified as early," Solena grumbled.

"We can go to the mall tomorrow. I still have some Christmas shopping to do and we can look for perfume then. And if we get there when it opens, it'll be less crowded. I mean, can you imagine how busy it is this time of day?"

Solena fumbled in her purse for her car keys. "Okay, but I want to be there when they open the doors tomorrow."

"I'll pick you up," Julie said, seeing Solena off.

Once Solena was gone, Julie changed into jeans and a sweater and grabbed her coat. "I'm out of here, Mom," she hollered, banging the storm door as she left.

It had snowed the night before, but the plows had cleared and salted the streets and traffic flowed smoothly. Julie drove across the railroad tracks that divided the city of Waterton and soon reached Luke's neighborhood. The houses were older and smaller here, clumped together, so that there were almost no side yards between them. The homes were close to the mill and changed owners frequently as the mill hired and laid off through the years.

Several homes were in need of repair. Luke's house needed a coat of paint, but still it looked tidy and neat compared with that of a neighbor, who had old cars partially torn down in his front yard. In the cool light of winter, the block seemed shabby and dismal.

Julie parked in the driveway and Luke met her on the porch. He gave her a quick kiss. "Mom took the afternoon off from work and she's cooking up a feast."

Inside, the smell of bubbling spaghetti sauce made Julie's mouth water. She followed Luke into the kitchen, where his mother was stirring a pot on the stove. "It smells wonderful," Julie exclaimed.

Nancy Muldenhower put down her wooden spoon, wiped her hands on a dish towel, and hugged Julie warmly. "I'm glad you could come for supper. Although it won't be ready for another three hours." She shot Luke a glance. "He insisted that you had to come this afternoon so that you could drive him somewhere. Why isn't Luke driving? What's going on with you two?"

Her lively brown eyes, so much like Luke's, caused Julie to grow flustered. "He's keeping a promise to me," Julie said hastily.

"What promise?"

"We'll tell you at supper," Luke interjected, getting Julie off the hook. Looking at Julie, he said, "Let me get some things out of my room and then we'll split."

Julie sat in a yellow kitchen chair to wait. The kitchen table looked scarred, battle-weary from years of service.

"Luke says you two are planning to stop by tomorrow night before the dance so I can see your dress."

"Yes . . . on our way to pick up Solena and Frank."

"It's nice of your father to lend Luke his car for the evening. Mine's not much newer than Luke's."

Julie's dad had made the offer weeks before and Luke had been thrilled over the prospect of driving the sporty auto. Julie would have been just as happy in Luke's car, but no one had asked her opinion. "Well, you know how Dad feels about Luke."

"He's been very good to my boy, and I'll always be grateful for the way he's taken him under his wing. It's not easy raising a boy without a father—especially in this neighborhood. I'd have moved years ago if I could have afforded it."

Julie thought Luke's mother was attractive, even if she was on the heavy side. Luke had always been protective of her, careful not to cause her worry or problems, which was part of his refusal to keep returning to the doctor for his unremitting flu bug.

"I like your house," Julie said. "It's cozy."

"It's old." Nancy stirred the sauce again and tapped the wooden spoon on the side of the pot. "We're putting up our Christmas tree next week. You will come and help decorate it, won't you?"

"Of course. How else can we keep Luke from slinging the tinsel on it?"

The two of them were laughing when Luke came back to the kitchen, ready to leave. "Why do I get the feeling you're laughing at me?"

After Nancy and Julie had poked some more good-natured fun at him, Luke promised his mother to return by five and he and Julie left the warm kitchen. Julie drove and Luke stared pensively out the window. "It's only a follow-up visit to your doctor," she chided, knowing instinctively how keeping the appointment was bothering him.

"I think it's a waste of time and money. I've been feeling better, you know."

"But you're not completely well." She thought he still looked thin, and she could see his gland protruding from beneath his jaw. "Maybe you have mono," she suggested. "You know—the 'kissing disease'?"

He grimaced. "That would be terrible. I'll have to give up kissing you."

"I haven't caught anything from you yet. If it's mono, I'll wear a mask." She grinned. "Come on, lighten up. This'll be over in no time. And tomorrow night we go to the dance and I'm going to look so good, it'll blow your socks off."

"Too late—you already blow my socks off."

The doctor's waiting room was crowded with sniffling kids and crying babies. A few adults sat with their heads buried in their hands, looking feverish. "If you're not sick, you will be by the time you're done sitting around this place," Luke grumbled.

"Stop grousing," Julie said. "Be a good sport."

Julie flipped through magazines while Luke fidgeted and watched the clock. Over thirty minutes passed before he was finally called into one of the waiting rooms. Another forty-five minutes passed and Julie grew restless herself. She imagined Luke forgotten in some cubicle, getting angry while he waited. Forty minutes later, the outer door opened and Luke's mother hurried inside.

"Nancy! Why are you here?"

"The doctor called and told me to come. I didn't know you were taking Luke to the doctor, Julie. Why didn't either of you tell me?"

"Luke didn't want to worry you."

"What's wrong with Luke? He wasn't sick when he left home."

At a loss for words, embarrassed, Julie shrugged.

An inner door opened and a nurse called them in. Quickly, they followed the woman down a narrow hall and into an office where a doctor sat behind his desk, writing in a file folder. Luke sat stiffly in a side chair. "Luke, are you all right?" His mother rushed toward him. Julie followed, hanging back slightly.

"I don't know." Luke sounded sullen. "Ask him."

The doctor stood and nodded. "I'm Dr. Portage."

"I'm Julie Ellis, his, uh . . . friend."

"I'm his mother. Where's Dr. Simms?"

"He's taken me on as his assistant."

"Tell me what's wrong."

Dr. Portage sat and steepled his fingers together. "I've checked Luke over, listened to his symptoms, and done some preliminary blood work. As I told you on the phone, I'm concerned about his elevated white blood count."

Julie felt her heart pounding and reached for Luke's hand. "Luke, he's scaring me."

Luke looked away. His hand felt cold as ice.

"I don't mean to alarm any of you," Dr. Portage said. "But I don't like what I'm seeing. I suspect Luke has some kind of infection. According to his records, he's been treated with antibiotics, but he hasn't responded as he should have."

"Are you saying you'll have to run more tests?" Nancy asked.

"Yes. And he needs to be in the hospital in order to run them. I've got a call in to St. Paul's Hospital in Chicago."

"Why Chicago? What's wrong with Waterton General?"

"They don't have the equipment and staff I want for Luke."

Julie and Luke exchanged glances. His dark eyes bored into her, making her even more afraid. "What do you mean?" Julie asked. Her voice quivered.

Dr. Portage looked directly at Luke. "I want you to go home, pack a bag, and drive straight to St. Paul's."

5

L uke jumped to his feet. "Right now? You want me go check in right *now?* No way!"

"The sooner the better," the doctor said.

"Now, Luke, we should do what the doctor says," his mother added.

"But the dance is tomorrow night."

"I don't care about the dance," Julie interjected.

"Well, I do."

The doctor's phone rang. He spoke quietly into the receiver, hung up, and told Luke, "That was St. Paul's. It's all arranged. You're to check in this afternoon, as soon as possible."

The remainder of the afternoon passed in a surrealistic blur for Julie. And while she would not recall later the exact sequence of events, she'd never forget the cold, snakelike fear that clutched at her insides and numbed her soul. She cried when she called her father on the phone from Luke's house. She found comfort in his absolute refusal to believe that the doctor was anything but "an incompetent fool who's allowed Luke's flu to get out of control and now has to cover his mistakes by subjecting Luke to useless testing."

"I'm going with them to St. Paul's, Dad."

"Maybe I should drive over too."

She knew he was preparing his presentation for the school board about the new stadium. "Why don't I call you from the hospital once I find out what's going on."

"All right. You stay with Luke's mom. She'll need someone."

Afterward, Julie watched Luke and his mother pack a duffel bag, her hands stiff with concern, his jerking with pent-up anger. Julie rode with them on the sixty-mile trip from Waterton to Chicago, and once inside the mammoth hospital, she sat with Luke in the patient admitting room, listening to Luke's mother answer countless questions and watching her fill out long insurance forms.

Julie took the elevator with Luke, his mom,

and a nurse to the sixth floor and accompanied them to the hospital room, where two beds, two bureaus, and two nightstands filled the space. All that separated the beds was a thin, pale green curtain. Luke was the only occupant, but the nurse told them that another patient could be checked in at any time and become Luke's roommate.

The nurse chattered cheerfully—Julie assumed to make them feel at ease. She told about the hospital routine, meals, TV, visiting hours. She said lab technicians would come to draw blood and do simple routine procedures. She told them that Dr. Portage would be in later that evening to see Luke and that he'd have a colleague, Dr. Sanchez, with him.

The nurse gave them more forms and instructions on how to find the nearby Ronald McDonald House, the facility where families of sick children could stay to be near their kids. Luke said, "I'm not a child. And I don't plan to be here too long."

And the nurse replied, "I'm just giving information."

"How long will he have to stay?" Nancy asked.

"That's up to his doctors."

Julie's head swam with information, jumbled emotions, the foreign smells of antiseptics, floor wax, and antibacterial soaps. She felt like a bird pushed helter-skelter by some strange air current. She felt so sorry for Luke she wanted to cry, and her eyes burned with unshed tears.

"I'm sorry about the dance," he said when his mother had gone with the nurse to take care of more details.

"The dance is nothing. All that matters is you getting well."

"There's nothing wrong with me except that I'm run-down. It's all some stupid mistake. Dr. Portage just got alarmed because he didn't cure me the first time."

"That's what Dad says. He wants to come see you."

"Not tonight. He's my coach, Julie. I don't want him to see me like this."

"I won't be able to keep him away."

Luke twisted his bedcovers, wadding them in his large fists. "Will you make sure Mom gets home all right?"

"I'll watch out for her. And I'll come back with her tomorrow."

He stared out the lone window. Night had come, and the darkness looked cold and brittle. "I hate this, Julie. I really hate this."

"It'll be over soon." She wanted so much to cheer him up. "You'll be back home and it'll be Christmas and New Year's and then school will start again. Everything's going to be okay."

She hugged him, locking her arms around his body. They held on to each other until his mother returned. She hugged him too and said she'd be back first thing in the morning. Julie and Luke's mother walked to the doorway, where they turned and waved. Julie's gaze lingered longingly on Luke's face. He smiled and flashed them a thumbs-up.

His expression was confident, identical to the one he wore during a football game against a superior foe. Julie had seen such bravado in his eyes a hundred times. Yet this time, she saw one more thing in their dark depths. She saw fear.

"There's no way I'm not going to spend the week over there with Luke's mother, Mom." Julie stood facing her mother defiantly in the middle of the kitchen floor, two days later.

"But it's almost Christmas, Julie, and we haven't even put up our tree."

"How can I think about Christmas with Luke going through all those tests in the hospital? Mrs. Muldenhower and I can stay together at the Ronald McDonald House and be with Luke every day. And that's where I want to be."

"Honey, I'm concerned about him too, but it's not like he's family. . . ."

Julie felt anger, hot and violent, simmering in her blood. She wanted to scream at her mother.

"Calm down," she heard her father say. He turned to his wife. "Be rational, Patricia. Of course Julie wants to be with Luke. That hospital is the pits for an active kid like Luke. And the tests they're fixing to give him could make a grown man cower."

Patricia Ellis stamped her foot. "Stop ganging up on me. I know he's your prized player, Bud. And I know he's Julie's boyfriend. But it's Christmas, for heaven's sake. Julie should be here with us."

"By Christmas Day, Luke will be home," Julie insisted. "And until he is, I'm packing some things and staying with him. And you can't stop me!" She spun on her heel, but her father stepped into the doorway, blocking her way.

"Watch your temper," he warned. He looked over her head at his wife. "You're wrong on this, Pat. Julie should be with Luke and his mother. And I'll be going over most days for visits, so I'll keep a check on her. Luke's a fine kid, and he shouldn't have to go through this by himself."

With her father's help, Julie had won the battle, and when Luke's mother arrived an hour later, Julie was packed and waiting by the front door. In Chicago, they checked in at the Ronald McDonald House, a modern facility with beautiful sleeping rooms, a huge living room and TV area, a modern, fully stocked kitchen, laundry facilities, and a large play-room for younger brothers and sisters of pa-tients at St. Paul's.

Julie and Nancy unpacked quickly, then hurried the two blocks to the hospital. They arrived at Luke's room in time for his return from radiology. "What did they do to you?" Julie asked anxiously.

"A CT scan," he said.

"Did it hurt?"

"Not a bit. They shoved me inside this huge machine and took an X ray of my entire body. The worst part was having to lie per-fectly still while they did it."

"What's the X ray for?"

"To see my glands on the inside." He gave

her a sidelong glance. "Maybe I'll start glowing in the dark."

"Very funny."

His mother kissed his forehead. "One of the nurses said Dr. Sanchez was on the floor. I'm going to find him and talk to him. Be right back."

When she'd gone, Luke opened his arms and Julie leaned over the bed to receive his hug. "I've missed you," he whispered against her ear.

"Oh, Luke, I've missed you too. I wish I could take you home with me right now."

"Why don't we make a dash for it? They won't notice until suppertime."

She laughed. At least he was in better spirits.

"Any feedback about the dance from Solena?" he asked.

"She and Frank missed us going with them."

"You didn't get to wear your new dress."

"I'll wear it to the next dance for you."

"Maybe we can go someplace special New Year's Eve. Would you like that?"

"Sure. But before we make any plans maybe we'd better see how all these tests come out."

He looked downcast. "I just want my life back."

She quickly searched for a way to distract him. "Did Dad tell you that the school board put off their vote on the new stadium until the middle of February?"

"He mentioned it when he was visiting yesterday. He was mad about it, wasn't he?"

"You know my dad," Julie said. "He doesn't *wait* too easily. He wants that stadium and he wants it *now!*" She banged her closed fist on the bedside table in an imitation of her father. "He says that if the school board doesn't get cracking, they won't break ground for it this spring."

"It'll get built," Luke said.

"I know. But he has his heart set on you playing in it your senior year."

Luke sighed. "Right now, I feel too weak to *pick up* a football, much less think about playing a *game.*"

"You'll feel better soon."

"I hope so." He held up his hand, which was fastened to an IV line. "They're pumping me full of antibiotics, but they don't seem to be helping much. I feel like a pincushion. Every day the lab takes blood. This is a real drag, Julie."

While Julie was trying to think of something to say to cheer him up, Luke's mother returned. Her face looked calm, yet Julie suspected she was upset. "I cornered that doctor of yours, and he said that they're going to take you into surgery tomorrow and do a biopsy on the gland in your neck."

"Surgery?" Julie felt her knees go weak. "You mean they're going to operate on Luke?"

"It's only a biopsy," Luke's mother said, trying to make it sound like a simple routine. "They'll take out some of the cells and send them to the lab for analysis. And they'll do a bone marrow biopsy at the same time."

"What are they looking for?" Luke asked the question without emotion.

"I'm not certain," Nancy said. But Julie could tell by the look in her eyes that she had a suspicion. One that she wasn't about to reveal. And one that, whatever it was, frightened her very much.

6

The biopsy procedure was indeed simple. Luke went down to the surgical floor at seven the next morning and was back in his room by nine. Both Julie's parents drove to Chicago to wait with Julie and Nancy, and afterward they all trooped in to see Luke as soon as he was brought up from recovery.

"You don't seem groggy from the anesthetic," Julie's mother observed. "When I had Julie, I was sick for three days from the stuff they gave me to put me to sleep."

"The anesthesiologist said that I would come out of it pretty fast, and he was right. I feel pretty good. Except that my neck hurts. And my hip's sore too." He touched the large white bandage taped to his neck and patted the covers atop his hips.

"That's because of the bone marrow aspiration. They inserted a syringe into your bone marrow and drew some out for testing," his mother explained. "Do you need some pain medication?"

Bud Ellis announced cheerily, "Luke's no *wimp*. He's used to taking hard hits on the football field, so a little slice out of his neck and a sore spot on his body won't set him back much."

"I only take hits if my defense fails to block their tackles," Luke said, making light of his discomfort.

It bothered Julie that he had to put on some macho act for her father, but she didn't say anything because she didn't want to embarrass him. As soon as her father left, she'd make certain that he got a pain pill from the nurse.

"What's next?" Coach Ellis asked.

Nancy responded with, "The full pathology report on the lump will be available in a couple of days; then Dr. Sanchez will know what we're dealing with."

"So, you'll probably be home for Christmas after all," Patricia Ellis said. "That'll be good." She paused, then added, "You know, I was wondering if the two of you might like to come over for Christmas dinner."

Julie was positively shocked. Her mother had never issued such an invitation before. Of course, Luke had eaten with her family on occasion, but never with his mom as a guest too.

"Are you sure?" Nancy asked, looking hesitant. "I've been so preoccupied with all of this that I haven't given Christmas a second thought. It would be very kind of you to have us."

"We're absolutely sure," Coach interjected.

"No need for both of us to cook," Patricia added.

Julie wondered if this was something her mother had come up with on her own or if her father was responsible for the invitation. At the moment, she didn't care. The thought of having Luke at her family's table for Christmas dinner would help her get through the ordeal of the hospital.

"Thanks, Mrs. Ellis," Luke said. He always called her "Mrs. Ellis" because she treated him rather formally. It irked Julie that her mother didn't adore Luke the way she and her father did, but she'd learned to live with it.

"I know it can't be fun being stuck in the hospital all during your holiday break," Julie's mother said.

"As word's gotten around, some of the guys on the team have called me. A few are going off on skiing trips with their families and staying at fancy resorts. I tell them that this is my resort for the holidays."

The adults laughed and the coach tapped Luke's shoulder. "That's the spirit. I knew they couldn't keep you down."

Later, when he and Julie were alone, Luke confided, "I wasn't exactly honest with your father. All this stuff *is* getting me down."

"It's okay to tell him. You don't always have to act as if you're in complete control."

"No, it's not okay. He expects me to blow this off and not get depressed."

"I know he does. And it makes me mad."

Luke looked surprised. "Why?"

"Because you shouldn't have to hide what you're really feeling for fear that it might disappoint someone."

"Don't be mad."

Unexpectedly, tears sprang to her eyes. "Well, I am. I'm mad because this is happening to you and you didn't do anything to deserve it. And I'm mad because people—especially my father—are acting like you shouldn't be too bothered by any of it. That's so lame! If it were me, I'd be throwing things at everybody who stuck his head in the door. Nurses, doctors, lab techs—everybody."

Luke grinned and took her hand. "Don't think I haven't wanted to. But I figure they're all only doing their jobs. Besides, don't forget—I'm a lover, not a fighter." He winked and she returned his smile. He said, "I got you a present."

"Me? But when, and how?"

He opened the drawer to his bedside table and extracted a long-stemmed red rose, wrapped in cellophane and tied with a bright green Christmas bow. He handed her the flower. "When I was in the recovery room, I begged one of the nurses to buy it for me in the gift shop and put it in my room so I could give it to you."

A lump of emotion clogged Julie's throat. "You're the one who's sick. *I* should be buying *you* flowers."

He shook his head, looking pleased by the reaction his unexpected gift had caused. "I'd rather have tickets to the Super Bowl."

She hugged him, holding him tightly and with great feeling. "Oh, Luke, I can't wait until all this is over."

"Me too," he said into her ear. "The only thing that's made it halfway tolerable is that you're here with me. Just a few more days, honey. Just a few more days."

The afternoon Dr. Sanchez came to discuss Luke's diagnosis with Luke, his mother, and Julie, the nurses were decorating the floor for the holidays. The scents of pine and bayberry filled the halls and each door was garnished with colorful ribbons. But when the doctor came inside the room, he closed the door and shut out the noise of Christmas preparations. The sun slanted through the blinds, casting patterns across Luke's bedcovers. The doctor, his hands full of charts and papers, pulled a chair to the side of the bed. Nancy sat near the doctor and Julie remained in her perch on the bed, her fingers laced through Luke's. The adjoining bed was still empty, so there was no one to overhear, no one to shut out with the flimsy green curtain.

"You're not smiling, Doc," Luke said. "Did the nurses forget to invite you to their Christmas party?"

"No way. Who do you think plays Santa Claus for the pediatric ward?" His banter was easy, but Julie saw that his eyes weren't smiling.

"So, what do you have to tell us?" Luke's mother asked. "What's wrong with my son?"

The doctor flipped open the manila folder on his lap. "I'm going to give this to you straight, Luke, because you asked me to."

"Yes, I did."

"And because it's the only way I deal with my patients. I talk straight."

Julie's heart began to hammer and her fingers tightened around Luke's.

"The official name for what you have is Hodgkin's Lymphoma."

Julie heard Luke's mother gasp and saw her shake her head. "What's that?" Julie asked, not one bit embarrassed by her ignorance.

"It's a form of cancer that develops in the lymph system, which is part of the body's circulatory system. Right now, you're in an early stage and your prognosis is good."

Cancer! Julie felt as if someone had hit her hard in the stomach and knocked the wind out of her. Maybe she hadn't heard Dr. Sanchez correctly. "But Luke's so healthy," she blurted. "He plays football."

"Hodgkin's is rare—it accounts for less than one percent of all cancer cases. Unfortunately, when we see it, it's in young people between the ages of fifteen and thirty-five. Basically, as in all cancers, the cells of the lymph system go crazy and start dividing at will. This breaks down the immune system—your body's infection-fighting machine—and it can spread to other organs."

Luke's face looked impassive, as if he were listening to a weather report. Julie wanted to scream, *No! No! You've made a mistake!*

"He never complained of any pain," Nancy said.

"His symptoms were classic—swollen, painless nodes in his neck, night sweats, fevers, weight loss. But those symptoms could be ascribed to any number of illnesses. That's why we ran so many tests." Dr. Sanchez removed several papers from the file folder.

"Your pathology report shows that the cells in your neck were positive for cancer. But on the good side, your CT scan showed that your lymph network looks clean. And your bone marrow biopsy was negative also. In other words, the cancer hasn't spread yet."

" 'Yet'?" It was the first time Luke had spoken.

"Untreated, it will spread."

"How do you treat it?" Luke asked.

"We start with chemotherapy."

Julie felt sick to her stomach. She'd heard about chemotherapy and its side effects.

Dr. Sanchez continued. "I'm moving you up to the oncology floor and assigning you another doctor. Paul Kessler is one of our top oncologists—a big football fan, too. He played for Duke University as an undergraduate. You'll like him."

"So I won't be home for Christmas." Luke's voice sounded flat. "You told me I'd be home for Christmas."

"You might be," Dr. Sanchez said. "Chemo patients are given their initial doses in the hospital to see how they tolerate the drugs and to work out the best combination. We'll insert a Port-A-Cath here." He touched an area near Luke's collarbone. "It's a tube gizmo surgically implanted under the skin so that your chemo can be administered without having to stick you all the time. The catheter's opening will be on the outside.

"Medications will be inserted every three weeks for six cycles, for a total of eighteen weeks. At that rate, you'll be through chemo by April."

"I've got to walk around with a stupid tube hanging half out of me? I've got to take all these weird chemicals? What about school? What about my *life?*" Luke's voice rose.

"Dr. Kessler will answer all your questions. Chemo is his specialty. But you'll be able to return to school once you're on the program. And after you adjust, you'll resume regular life. The chemo treatments will eventually be over, Luke."

Luke's face had become an angry mask and his hand in Julie's felt icy cold. "And then what, Doc? Will the cancer be gone forever? Will I get to pick up where I left off? Or is this thing going to hang over me for the rest of my life?"

"I can't answer that, Luke. I don't know."

"Well, maybe I don't want to go through chemo and all. Maybe I just want to pack up and go home and forget the whole mess."

"Luke, you can't—" his mother began.

The doctor interjected, "You have the right to refuse treatment, Luke, but it wouldn't be wise. With it, you at least have hope for recovery. Without it, you will most certainly die."

7

Nothing had prepared Julie for Luke's diagnosis. She moved through the next day in a numbing fog of disbelief. She sobbed into the phone when she told her father and felt an odd kind of comfort in his display of explosive anger. Her mother was sympathetic, and sorry, but she wanted Julie to come home—Christmas was only a week away. Julie refused, becoming adamant about staying with Luke's mother at the Ronald McDonald House. She couldn't leave Luke. She simply couldn't.

He was started on chemo, and the side effects were immediate. He began vomiting continually. "It takes some adjustments to arrive at the right combination," Dr. Kessler said. "The important thing is, Luke has to keep eating."

His advice seemed stupid, since Luke couldn't keep anything down. Luke begged Julie to go home. "I don't want you to see me like this," he moaned. His skin looked ashen.

"I'm not leaving," Julie insisted. Yet, the weekend before Christmas, she decided to return home long enough to replenish her wardrobe—and to appease her mother. She rode the high-speed train from Chicago to Waterton, where her father picked her up at the station.

"You look thin," he said.

"I'm fine," she told him.

Walking into her house, she felt like a stranger. The decorations were up. It was the first time in all of her seventeen years that she hadn't helped with the festivities. She went quickly to her room, and felt like a stranger there too. Everything was familiar, yet alien. She'd grown used to the hospital smells and sparse furnishings. Her room seemed too colorful. Too cluttered.

Julie kept a tight rein on her emotions as she dumped the contents of her suitcase on the bed and started toward her closet for fresh clothes. Midway, she stopped. Draped on a hanger from atop the molding of the closet door, exactly where she'd left it, was the black taffeta dress she was to have worn to the school holiday dance.

The dress looked beautiful and pristine. It reminded her of a simpler time, a throwback to days of unhurried sweetness when nothing was more pressing in her life than studying for a test. Or talking on the phone with Solena. Or making plans for a date with Luke. She felt a catch in her throat.

Slowly, she approached the dress and fingered the satiny material. How foreign it felt. Her hands were used to touching hospital sheets, hospital-issue pajamas, and cotton blankets. The dress's elegant fabric no longer belonged in her world. She wondered if there would ever be room for such an extravagance again.

Tears slid down her cheeks, wetting her skin. She felt her shoulders begin to shake as sobs, unchecked, poured out of her. *Luke, Luke . . . What's going to happen to us?* She couldn't stop crying. Couldn't stop aching inside. Julie buried her face in the dark fabric and felt the dampness soak into the material. She could almost hear her mother saying, "Be careful. Water will stain taffeta. It's not a very practical dress, you know."

But Julie only wept harder, not caring.

Somehow the tearstains seemed appropriate. The dress would wear the watermarks forever, a symbol of the lost innocence of her life. Of the cruel and bitter upheaval in Luke's. The dress was fantasy. The heap of practical clothing on her bed was real life.

Quickly, Julie jerked open the closet door and, with muffled weeping, began to repack.

On Christmas Day, Luke's hair began to fall out. "Ho, ho, ho," he said without mirth, holding up the wad of hair left on his pillow.

"It's only hair," Julie said. But inwardly, she was shaken.

At her mother's insistence—as well as Luke's and his mother's—she had gone home Christmas Eve and spent Christmas morning with her parents. Then, bringing gifts, she and her family had driven over to Chicago to visit Luke.

The hospital staff had done its best to make the day festive for the patients on the oncology floor, wheeling them out of their rooms to gather round the decorated tree in the rec room next to the nurses' station. They had bought and wrapped gifts for all their regulars, which Julie found touching. It struck her that in a weird way, they were all part of a family, one held together by the disease of cancer. Many of the patients were worse off than Luke, but he was the youngest one on the floor, and clearly a favorite of the staff.

Coach Ellis brought him a football signed by the players on the Indianapolis Colts, and she had given him a baseball hat, a sweater, and a glamorous color photograph of herself. He sat holding it, staring down at her smiling face. "You're beautiful, Julie. You look just like Marilyn Monroe."

"Oh, stop it," she chided, embarrassed by his compliment. He'd been a fan of Marilyn's for years; posters of her hung in his room beside posters of NFL superstars. "You told me once that you wanted a good picture of me, so I had it made for you. It's nothing special."

"It is to me." He looked into her eyes, and in spite of his gaunt face, his thinning hair, and his sallow complexion, she still considered him handsome. "I bought you this last October. I've been paying it off a little at a time. Mom got it out for me last week when she went home for the day." He handed her a small, wrapped box.

Inside was a gold bracelet, the chain thin and delicate, with tiny pearls set like staggered snowdrops along its length. She thought it was the most wonderful gift she'd ever received from him and told him so by kissing him in front of the entire assembly. Everybody clapped and Luke blushed. "I got you this too," he said, and produced a rose, which gave her another opportunity to kiss him.

That night, Julie and Luke's mother returned to their room at the Ronald McDonald House. Nancy put away her few gifts. Julie's parents had been generous to Luke's mother, buying her a stylish cable-knit sweater and a gift certificate to a Waterton area department store, which Julie had brought to Chicago.

"Being stuck in the hospital is a crummy way to spend the holiday," Julie announced as she climbed under the covers. "And I know the hospital kitchen tried, but my mom's Christmas dinner is so much better."

"Perhaps she'll give us a rain check on that dinner."

"I know she will."

"I can't thank you and your parents enough for all you've done for Luke and me. When Luke was younger, I was so afraid he'd take up with the wrong crowd. But then football came along, and with it, your dad. He's treated Luke like a son."

"Luke's never talked much about his father.

Not even to me. I guess he misses having one more than ever now."

"I don't think he remembers Larry very well."

"He died in a fall, didn't he?"

"Yes. He was walking the steel riggings. He'd only been on the job for a few months. The company paid his funeral expenses and I was lucky enough to be hired on as an office worker."

"Well, you're the office *manager* now," Julie said.

"It's taken me seven years of hard work to get there. That's why I want Luke to go to college."

Although Julie believed Nancy accepted the way she and Luke felt about one another, Julie also knew Nancy had dreams for her son. She prized education and always urged Luke to get good grades so that he could have a better life. In that respect, Nancy and Julie's mother thought alike. They equated getting out of Waterton with optimum happiness.

"You're lucky to have such a nice family, Julie. I wish I had more family around me. Especially now."

None of Luke's grandparents was living. "Luke's uncle Steve knows what's going on, doesn't he?" Steve was Luke's father's only brother.

"Yes, but he's all the way out in Los Angeles. Except for phone calls and cards, there's nothing he can do. We haven't seen him for years. He's a bachelor with a job connected to the movie industry. He has a life of his own out there. No . . . I'm afraid all Luke and I have for support is each other. And your family, of course. Your family has made all the difference in our lives, Julie."

Julie wondered if Nancy would be so comfortable if she understood how much Julie's mother wanted Julie and Luke's relationship to cool off. "I'll always be here for Luke," Julie declared. "No matter what."

Nancy smiled. "Right now, you're the only thing holding my son together. This chemo business has knocked him for a loop. Kids—boys especially—think they're invincible. Why, I can count on one hand the number of days Luke's been sick in his life. When he gets sick, he doesn't mess around with the small stuff, does he?"

Tears filled Nancy's eyes and Julie thought she might break down. "The chemo treatments won't last forever," Julie said hastily.

Nancy sniffled hard. "And he isn't nearly as sick as he was in the beginning."

"Still, it's a crummy way to spend Christmas."

"A crummy way," Nancy echoed.

Their conversation had come full circle. They gave each other a good-night hug, turned off the lights, and went to bed. Julie lay in the dark staring at the window. Even though the curtains were closed, she could see the faint outline of Christmas lights aglow in nearby buildings. Their soft colors reminded her of her tree back home and filled her with longing to be a kid again. To be exhausted from getting up too early to see what Santa had brought. To be full of Christmas dinner and too much candy. To be snuggled in her own bed, in her own room, with nothing to think about but playing with her new toys when morning came.

But she wasn't a little girl anymore. And this Christmas, she was miles from home, in a rented room, with a hospital a block away. With Luke, the only boy she'd ever loved, receiving chemo for a rare and deadly form of cancer. She fingered the bracelet on her wrist and stuffed her fist into her mouth, so that Nancy wouldn't hear her cry herself to sleep.

8

D r. Kessler allowed Luke to return home New Year's Day. Luke was to remain on chemo for another week, then go off treatment for two weeks, then begin the process all over again.

"The county can get you tutors so that you can stay on grade level," Julie heard her mother, who had brought a casserole to Luke's house for dinner that night, tell him.

"I might want a tutor," he said. "I'd really like to stay caught up with my class."

Until then, it hadn't occurred to Julie that Luke might not go back to school. The term started the next day and she had to return. "You should come to school," Julie said once her mother was gone. "Everybody's asking about you. You'll feel better seeing the gang."

"I don't know," he said. "I look pretty

grim." He wore his baseball cap all the time to hide his bald head.

"Not to me."

"Then you'd better get glasses." He sighed and flopped back against the couch. "I look like a freak, Julie. And I feel like one too." He pulled the neck of his sweater up higher, making certain it covered the catheter near his collarbone.

"You can't stay out the entire term," Julie insisted.

"When I'm off chemo, I might consider going back. But once I start treatments again, I'll have to drop out. I don't want to start barfing in the classroom."

"Not even in Ms. Tyler's?" She named the most formidable English teacher at the high school.

He ignored her attempt to be funny. "Don't pressure me. This isn't something I can decide now. Will you come over tomorrow afternoon and tell me about your day?"

"Sure," she said, but she was disappointed. Somehow, she'd assumed that once he got out of the hospital, he'd act more like his old self.

Julie returned to Waterton High and was bombarded with questions about Luke all day long. Students, teachers, even the principal and office personnel queried her. In the cafeteria with Solena, she could hardly get her lunch down for the interruptions.

"Frank says that the guys on the team want to do something for Luke, but they don't know what," Solena said after the crowd momentarily cleared away from the table. "Some of the guys are weirded out about it. They think Luke hung the moon and they can't imagine him being sick this way."

"Then fire up your imagination—he really is."

"But *cancer!* It—it's so *unfair!*"

"Please, Solena, don't talk about it. I know it's unfair, and I get mad whenever I think about it. So why don't we just change the subject, all right?"

Solena looked contrite. Julie heard the drone of nearby voices, the clatter of silverware, the clack of plates being scraped and stacked. After a few minutes of awkward silence, Solena said, "Frank's taking me into Chicago Friday night for a concert. I wish you and Luke could come with us. We haven't doubled in ages—it would be like old times."

"Well, we can't." Julie hadn't meant for her voice to sound so sharp, but Solena was getting on her nerves.

"What are you going to do with yourself?"

"What do you mean?"

"Will you . . . you know . . . date anybody else?"

"How could you suggest such a thing? I would never run around on Luke. Especially now."

"I—I didn't mean get *serious* with anybody else, but golly, Julie, what are you going to do Friday and Saturday nights? Just sit at home? Or go over to Luke's all the time?"

Julie hadn't thought that far ahead, but all at once she saw the weeks stretching in front of her in one long, monotonous string. With Luke sick and not willing to come out of his shell, there'd be no dates, no special events in their lives. The thought upset her. And she was upset with Solena for making her think about it. "He won't be sick forever," Julie snapped. "As soon as he's finished with his chemo treatments, he'll be well and he can pick up his life again."

"That's good. I was hoping everything would get back to normal for the two of you."

Normal. After so many weeks of being in the grip of crisis, Julie had forgotten what "normal" felt like. Suddenly, she felt depressed. But she also saw that she couldn't allow Luke to retreat from the world, for both of their sakes. If she loved him, she'd do her best to help him resume a normal existence. And if he loved her, he'd do it.

She discussed it with her father, and two days later Julie was at Luke's watching an afternoon TV game show with him when her dad arrived carrying a large box.

"What's up, Coach?" Luke asked as Bud Ellis set the box in the center of the floor, right in front of the television screen.

"I brought you a little present." He proceeded to open the box and to lift out shiny new barbells and weights. "You know that the guys on the team are hitting the weight room regularly."

"Sure. We—they do every year."

"Well, I figure you won't be going to the gym right away for workouts, but I don't want my number one quarterback turning into a glassy-eyed wimp." He cast a disdainful glance toward the TV. "I want you on a weight-lifting program, Luke."

"Gee, Coach, I don't know . . ."

Julie held her breath. She saw the struggle Luke was having stamped visibly on his face. He didn't want to let her father down. But he was also very unsure of his abilities.

"Luke, I don't expect you to bench-press two hundred pounds the way you were when the season ended. This stuff is just to get you started, keep you from falling too far behind. Start slow. Do arm curls with low weights." He fitted five-pound disks onto a set of barbells as he talked. "Do three sets of twelve four times a day until you feel stronger. I'll work with you."

Julie could see the muscle along Luke's jaw working and knew he was clenching his teeth. "Don't you want to play next season?" she asked.

"I haven't thought about anything else," he said quietly. "Football means everything to me."

"Then let's get you started on a program to build you back up," Bud said.

"I feel pretty lousy, Coach."

"I know, son." He reached out and gripped Luke's shoulder. "But you will feel better. You're going to lick this thing, Luke. You're going to get well and you're going to play football in your senior year. And every college coach in the country is going to sit up and take note."

Julie saw the fire of longing flicker in Luke's brown eyes. It caused a lump in her throat as she realized how long it had been since she'd seen it there. She was grateful to her father for igniting it. "I'll help, Luke," she said. "When you're strong enough to run laps, I'll clock you. I'll even run with you."

He gave her a partial smile. "What if you beat me?"

"I can keep my mouth shut. I won't blab it around."

He reached down and gripped the thick steel middle of the bar, and slowly, he lifted it, curling it up to his chest. "Man, I'm weak as a kitten."

"But the muscle's still there," Coach said. "All you have to do is tone it, build it up. You can do it, Luke. I remember that scrawny little kid who first reported to the Y locker room when he was twelve. Why, I was sure a big puff of wind would blow him over."

Luke smiled. "I wasn't much, was I?"

"What you lacked in build, you made up for in determination. I never saw a kid as determined as you. You spent months in the weight room bulking up. And more months practicing throwing the football."

"You still think I'll have what it takes to play?"

"You've always had what it takes: determination plus hard work."

"Lots of guys work hard at the game. And you're a good coach."

"But you've also got talent, Luke. I can't put into any player something God left out."

Luke's gaze skimmed the weights strewn around the carpet. "I guess I could give it a try. The days get pretty long with nothing to do but feel punk and do schoolwork."

"That's the spirit," Coach Ellis said, beaming him a smile. "After I wrap up my duties at school, I'll head over here and we'll get to work."

"I do want to play again," Luke said wistfully.

"And you will," Julie's dad insisted, giving Julie a sly wink.

She smiled, feeling optimistic that Luke would soon get his zest back. She was appreciative of her father's actions and saw with clarity one of the reasons he was such a good coach: he inspired and motivated a person; he didn't threaten and intimidate.

And she made up her mind that she wasn't going to sit around feeling sorry for herself because she had to stay home on a Friday or Saturday night. As long as Luke was sick, she'd be there for him. By spring, this whole chemo business would be behind him and they could get on with their lives. And she was now more positive than ever that whatever Luke Muldenhower did with his life, she wanted to be right by his side doing it with him.

She reached over and laced her fingers through Luke's. "If you're going to pump iron, I will too."

Luke and her father glanced at each other.

"I'm serious," Julie said. "What's the matter? Can't stand a little competition?"

Luke tweaked the muscle in her upper arm and rolled his eyes.

"Very funny," Julie sniffed.

But her father broke out in a roaring laugh and Luke's smile lit up his face. Julie thought the sight so beautiful that she didn't mind one bit being the focus of their joke. No, not one tiny little bit.

9

Eventually, Luke decided to return to school. Julie was proud of him, for she knew it wasn't easy. He'd always been admired at Waterton High and looked up to by both students and faculty. He was handsome, the star quarterback, a good student, and an all-around nice guy. But cancer and chemotherapy had left their mark.

There were those who whispered about the change in him. The girls were the worst. Julie would swing into the bathroom between classes and conversation would stop as all eyes turned toward her. She'd know they'd been discussing Luke, and she disliked them for it—would glare at them, daring them to continue with their gossip.

His baseball hat became a familiar sight in the halls and classrooms. No teacher ever asked him to remove it. Often, because he was so tall, Julie could see the hat bobbing above the crush of bodies passing from room to room between classes.

In a show of camaraderie, the players on the football team bought matching baseball hats and wore them every day. Even Julie's dad wore one, and one day the local paper came out and did a story about Luke and the symbol of the hats.

On the weeks he was on chemo, Luke wore bulky sweaters to hide the black pouch he strapped around his torso that controlled the flow of medications into the Port-A-Cath in his neck. If he felt nauseated in the classroom, he simply edged out the door and into the bathroom. He never had to ask permission. It was simply understood that if Luke needed to leave for a while, he was free to go.

He continued his weight regime, and slowly his muscles began to strengthen. He took special vitamins, protein powders, and high-energy drinks to maintain proper nutrition levels. He insisted on going to a tanning salon to give his sallow complexion a more vibrant and healthy look. One day Julie teased, "You'd better be careful, Beach Boy. The girls are starting to look hard at you, and I can't stand the competition."

"You have no competition," he said. "Never have. Never will." And to make his point, he had flowers delivered to her in the middle of a morning class.

By April, the last of the snow had finally melted and flowers had begun to bloom, first crocuses and jonquils, then tulips and lilies. Julie often found Luke after school sitting in the old bleachers overlooking the football field. She would climb up the weathered wooden slats and sit beside him, bringing him sometimes a candy bar, other times handfuls of foil-wrapped candy kisses. Chocolate seemed to be the one thing he could always keep down, no matter how sick the chemo made him.

"So what are you thinking about?" Julie asked as she settled next to him late one afternoon. A cool breeze was blowing. She hugged the letter jacket he had given her when they were freshmen tightly to her body.

"I'm thinking that spring's my favorite time of year," Luke told her. He was gazing thoughtfully out across the field. The grass looked hopelessly brown, but a few hardy dandelions had begun to dot the ground like bright yellow exclamations points.

"I don't believe it. You love football, and that's in autumn."

"Yeah, but before now, I took spring for granted. Everybody does, you know. They figure that it'll just wander in. But this year, it's extra special to me. And extra pretty."

"Why, Luke—you almost sound like a poet." She linked her arm through his.

"I'd write a poem if I could." He tossed back his head and breathed in deeply. "Everybody's always rushing around, Julie. They never stop and look around. They never see the new green color of the trees. Have you ever noticed how bright that shade of green is? And the flowers . . . flowers always seem to know when it's time to start growing. One day the ground is flat, and the next day little green stems are poking up. I've watched them for a week, so I know. They're asleep under the ground all through winter. Then they pop up."

She'd never heard him be so contemplative. "I guess we all take such things for granted. We figure, 'Spring came last year; it will this year too.'"

His gaze swept the area. "I'll never take it

for granted again. I'll always be grateful to see every spring that ever comes along."

She shivered, not from the cold, but from the tone of melancholy in his voice. "I will too."

He looked down at her. "So maybe this whole experience has made me more sensitive. What do you think?"

"I think I'd rather you not have had the experience and be less sensitive."

He laughed, and the sound thrilled her. He was beginning to seem so much more like his old self. "I start the final round of chemo next week. I didn't think I'd ever get to this point."

"And next Saturday is the sports banquet," she reminded him. The year-end awards banquet for the athletic department was to be held at Waterton's only resort hotel, built on the shore of Lake Michigan. Every athlete in the high school would be honored and over two hundred people were expected to attend. "Dad's talked about nothing else for days. You are taking me, aren't you?"

His expression clouded. "Julie, I don't know how I'll be feeling—"

She interrupted. "Poor excuse. We missed the Christmas dance and the Valentine's dance. We have to go to the banquet. I won't take no for an answer."

He was quiet.

She asked, "Luke, what's wrong? Why don't you want to go?"

"It's hard to be around the team, that's all."

"You see the guys every day at school. What's the difference?"

"The difference is I'll be on display. At school, I can just blend into the crowd. But the banquet will be full of parents and news people. I hate people staring at me, Julie . . . feeling sorry for me."

"People can't help but feel sorry. What happened to you stinks. But look how far you've come! People want to be happy for you too. They want to see you be the winner that you are."

He cocked his head. "Do you really believe I'm a winner?"

"I don't hang with losers."

"I love you, Julie."

She grinned. "Then I'll take that as a yes. You'll take me to the banquet?"

He slumped, feigning defeat. "Do you always get your way?"

"Of course—I'm Coach Ellis's daughter."

She looked at her watch. "Now let's get you home. It's time to begin your workout."

Hand in hand, they descended the bleachers and headed for the parking lot.

Julie had never seen her father so nervous as he was the night of the banquet. He kept tugging at the neck of his rented tux. "For heaven's sake, Bud, stop fidgeting," Julie's mother said. She wore a filmy black dress that Julie thought made her look sophisticated and pretty. "We've been going to these banquets for years. This one's no different."

"It is for me."

Julie was aware that something was going on. Her father had been acting secretive for days.

Patricia Ellis asked, "Do you have to wear that baseball cap tonight? It looks silly with the tux."

Julie butted in. "The whole team's wearing their caps, Mom, because Luke has to wear his. I think it's sweet." She smiled at her dad.

Her mother sighed. "Very well. Let's go. We promised Nancy we'd pick her up at five-thirty."

Julie's parents left and minutes later, Frank, Solena, and Luke drove up to her house. "You look good enough to kiss," Luke told her when she slid into the backseat of Frank's car.

"I'm puckered up."

He kissed her lightly. "I'm nervous," he confided. "People have been acting strange around me. Especially Frank." He nodded toward the back of Frank's head. The customary hat was pulled low over Frank's ears.

Solena glanced back and rolled her eyes. She was clearly disgusted with Frank, but Julie didn't care. She was glad the guys were wearing their matching caps.

The dining hall of the luxury hotel was packed with tables and crowded with people. Each sport had been granted a specific area of the great room. Football took up the largest space and was up front, near the podium. At the speakers' table, stretching across the front of the room, special dignitaries were seated. Julie waved to her parents, who were seated between the principal and school superintendent.

All through the meal and award presentations, Julie held Luke's hand under the table. She realized it was difficult for him to sit through the ceremony, knew that every award, every word of praise reminded him of the "before time"—before he got cancer. Luke was showered with certificates and trophies, including the prestigious Player of the Year, an award that usually went to a graduating senior, not a junior. But there was little doubt that he deserved it. Leading the team to the semifinals of the state championship was something no athlete from Waterton had done in over twenty-five years.

"We'll win it next year," Julie's father said into the mike as Luke made his way back to his seat carrying his trophy. The room erupted into cheers and shouts. Coach Ellis held up his hands for quiet. "I have a little something I want to show all of you," he said.

A curtain parted and two waiters carried out an easel. On it was a large, flat object covered with a velvet drape. "Ladies and gentlemen," Coach Ellis said with little fanfare, "I want to present the final drawings of the new Waterton Warriors football stadium."

He pulled off the drape and exposed a gorgeous artist's rendering of a brand-new stadium. The crowd applauded wildly. "We'll break ground this summer," the coach said. "And although it won't be completed until the following fall, it will be the best stadium with the finest playing turf in the state. In fact, we may play the state championships here in the future."

Again, wild applause. Julie squeezed Luke's hand. The stadium would not be ready in time for him to play in it, but it was still nice for her to see one of her father's dreams come true.

"Uh—Coach . . . ," Frank called, then stood up, walked swiftly to the front, and spoke into the mike. "The guys would like to say thanks for a great year." He handed Julie's dad a long white envelope, which Julie knew contained tickets for a night on the town in Chicago.

"And one more thing," Frank said.

In unison, the players stood. Mystified, Julie gave Luke a questioning look. Equally baffled, he shrugged.

"This is for you, Luke, buddy. It's a little present that the guys and Coach want to give you."

One by one, the team members removed their baseball caps to expose heads shaved perfectly bald. Every one of them, even her father, had shaved his head clean. People gasped, then began to applaud. Then they stood and looked toward Luke.

Julie rose to her feet, her gaze locked on

Luke's face, a lump the size of a fist lodged in her throat. She saw tears shimmering in his eyes. Then he too stood, swept off his hat from his smooth head, and bowed in tribute to the sacrifice his coach and friends had made in his honor.

10

Julie celebrated the completion of Luke's chemo by throwing a party, and she gave it the night her parents were to go into Chicago to use their banquet gift certificate.

"I'm not sure, Julie," her mother said when Julie told her the plans. "I hate to leave you and your friends unchaperoned."

"Mother, please." Julie sighed dramatically. "My friends know how to act. Most of them are Daddy's players; they're not going to get crazy or anything. Daddy would make their lives miserable."

"*No* alcohol," her mother said emphatically.

"Not to worry. Everybody wants Luke to have a good time and so I know they'll be on their best behavior."

"Is Solena going to help you?"

"Solena and a couple of others. We'll clean everything up. Don't worry."

So, her parents left in the early afternoon and Julie and her friends baked pizzas, made tacos, whipped up batches of chocolate chip cookies, hung lights on the back patio and deck, and set up two sets of stereo speakers—indoors and out. Just before six o'clock, the girls went up to Julie's room and got ready.

"Hair spray!" Solena shrieked. "I forgot my hair spray."

"Put a lid on it," Diane called. "Use mine."

Julie watched her friends running around and felt satisfaction. She thought back to those long days when Luke was in the hospital and recalled how much she had missed this kind of activity. One thing about the whole experience—it certainly made her more appreciative of everyday life. And grateful for life's "little things."

Although it was May, the evenings were still cool. Julie wore a dress and a lightweight sweater the same color as her eyes, and when Luke arrived with Frank, his expression told her that her choice had been perfect.

"Look at this," he said, and sweeping off his cap, he bent to show her the top of his head.

"There's black fuzz," she exclaimed.

He grinned. "I figure it'll soon be long enough for you to run your fingers through."

"Why wait?" she asked, and brushed her palm over the downy growth.

Frank was dancing past with Solena. "Make a wish," he called to Julie.

"I wish it'll grow so long so fast, he'll have to wear a ponytail to the first football practice."

"If any of us come to training camp next August with ponytails, your father will personally shave our heads again."

They laughed, and Julie leaned forward and placed a kiss on top of Luke's head. Her bright pink lipstick left a perfect imprint of her mouth.

"Oh, man!" Frank groaned in protest. "Wipe it off."

"Not a chance," Luke said. He took Julie's hand and led her out onto the deck, where music was playing and a few couples were slow-dancing. He took her in his arms. "It feels so good to hold you like this," he whispered in her ear.

A tingle shot up her spine as she realized how much she'd missed him. True, she'd been with him every day, but not like this. Not with him feeling well and wanting to act like a boyfriend again. "I promised my parents there wouldn't be any trouble," she said softly.

"What kind of trouble could this lead to?" He nuzzled her neck and her heart thudded expectantly.

"The kind where I lose my head and leave lipstick marks all over your body."

He chuckled. "Promises, promises."

"Don't test my patience, buster."

"How about if I test your endurance?" With that, he kissed her, holding his mouth to hers until she was dizzy.

The slow-dance music ended and another, faster song began. He broke the kiss and grabbed her hand. "Come on. Go for a walk with me."

They strolled down the sloping backyard, through the tender green shoots of new grass, until they reached the huge oak tree at the far end of the yard. He leaned against the tree and pulled her against him. She felt his hands smooth her hair and heard him breathe in its fragrance. "Oh, Julie . . . I'm so glad it's all over with."

She knew he was referring to his cancer treatments. "Me too."

"Of course, I still have to go for blood work

every six weeks for a while. And Dr. Kessler wants another CT scan the first of June."

"I'll go with you."

"I'll never forget the way you've stood by me."

She pulled away and realized he was being sincere. "Luke, I could never have left you alone in all this."

Doubt flicked across his face. "Sometimes, I was afraid you would. It couldn't have been much fun skipping stuff at school—the dances . . . basketball games. Guys would line up if they thought you were free of me, Julie."

"Line up for what? A rejection slip?" She reached up and traced her fingertips along a carving in the tree. "Remember doing this?"

He glanced over his shoulder and read, " 'LM plus JE.' I remember. I was twelve and I saw you out here with Tommy Fischer one afternoon. I got so jealous that late at night I sneaked into your yard and carved this into the tree."

"And when Tommy saw it, he knew immediately who LM was and he got so scared you'd beat him up that he ran off and never came over again." She poked Luke's chest and teased, "That wasn't very nice."

"You were so mad, you threatened to have your father throw me off his team." Luke grinned, remembering.

"And then you showed up on my porch holding that wad of flowers and you looked at me with those big brown eyes and I melted."

He grinned more broadly. "Once I discovered your weak spot, I never forgot."

She snuggled close again. "Lucky for you I'm not allergic to flowers."

She heard him sigh, heard the rumble of his heart against her ear, and thought she'd not been so content since before Christmas. "Did I tell you Uncle Steve called me?" he asked.

"When?"

"Last night."

"All the way from Los Angeles?"

"He was checking on me and Mom. He's a nice guy." Luke paused. "He's invited me out to visit him this summer."

"Really?" She was half glad, half sorry. "What did you tell him?"

"I said I wasn't sure. Of course, Mom wants me to go. You know how she feels about Waterton and getting out of this town."

"You should go," Julie said halfheartedly.

"I don't want to leave you."

She was touched, but thinking about all the

misery his illness had caused him, she knew she couldn't allow him to forgo the trip on her account. "You couldn't stay long anyway," she said. "Dad will expect you to show up on time for fall practice."

"What will you do this summer?"

"Mom's got me a job with her friend Mrs. Watson to help down at the public library." Julie wrinkled her nose. "She wants me to *work.*"

"That's a pretty good job." Summer jobs in a town the size of Waterton weren't plentiful, and Luke and Julie knew she was lucky to have one. Luke added, "Just think, you'll have some money to take me out."

"I'll have money to buy school clothes," she corrected.

"I'm wounded."

"Get over it." She patted his shoulder, then sobered. "Actually, I'm kind of provoked with my mom. She committed me to the job without even asking me first. But that's her style— jump in with both feet and make excuses if you have to back out."

"But you won't mind working there, will you? I mean, it beats schlepping groceries or baby-sitting."

"I guess not. Anyway, if you can go visit your uncle, you should."

"Will you write me?"

"Every day."

He rested his chin atop her head. "I'm going to start working out at the gym after school with the guys. I've got a lot of body-building to catch up on. Uncle Steve says he belongs to a gym and I can work out whenever I want if I come. I have to be in good shape by fall."

"If you're worried about losing your starting position, don't be," Julie said. "Dad's counting on you to lead the team."

"Maybe that's what's got me worried."

"How so?"

"He expects so much of me, Julie. I—I don't how much this problem's affected my game."

She understood his fears. Her father had a subtle way of applying pressure, of placing a mantle of expectation on his players that weighed heavily. No one ever wanted "to let Coach down."

Her mother often tried similar tactics on her, but she was not very subtle and usually it led to friction between them, rather than compliance. "You'll get your game back," Julie assured him. "My dad will see to it."

Luke grinned. "You're the only person in the world who can twist your father around her little finger."

"Don't you believe it. Daddy loves me, but we're both stubborn."

Luke looped his arms around Julie's waist. "You know what I think?"

"What?"

"I think this conversation has gotten too far afield. I brought you out here, away from all those partying people, to get your undivided attention."

"You've got it. What do you want?"

"This." He lowered his head and skimmed her mouth with his lips. Again, her knees went weak. "I love you, Julie."

"Talk is cheap," she whispered.

He straightened, reached into his jeans, and pulled out a pocketknife. "Then let me spell it out for you."

He dug the tip of the knife into the bark of the old tree, and soon, under their initials, symbols emerged—the letter I, a lopsided heart, and the letter U. He stepped back. "Now it's in writing for the whole world to see."

She draped her arms around his neck, rose on her tiptoes, and kissed the end of his nose. "For the whole world to see," she echoed. "The whole, entire world."

Julie, Luke, and his mother rode the train into Chicago the first Friday in June for testing. They had to take the train because Nancy's car was in the shop and Luke's was too old for such a trip. "I like the train," Nancy insisted.

Julie didn't mind it because she could cuddle with Luke while watching the scenery zip past. Eventually, trees and countryside gave way to buildings, parking lots, and malls.

At the hospital, Julie waited with Nancy while Luke went into the radiology department for the test. She tried to read a magazine, but couldn't concentrate.

When Luke came back, he told them, "Dr. Kessler wants us to wait while the radiologist reads the scan. He says it'll save us a trip back."

So they waited another hour, until Dr. Kessler's nurse called them up to his office on the seventh floor. They rode the elevator, Julie feeling as if her stomach were twisted in a knot. Perhaps it was just being back in the hospital that was making her nervous; she wasn't sure. All she knew was that she wanted to see a smile on Dr. Kessler's face and hear him give Luke a clean bill of health.

"The last time your scans were negative," Nancy said. "No reason they shouldn't be the same now."

But when they walked into Dr. Kessler's office, he wasn't smiling. Behind him, X rays were mounted on a light board so that they glowed clearly in dull gray and white.

"Is that me?" Luke asked.

"That's you," Dr. Kessler said. "And I'm afraid there's a problem. There's a mass in your chest."

11

"A mass?"

"A growth—a small tumor," the doctor said, tapping Luke's chest. "It's here on your left side, between your lung and your heart."

Instantly, Luke was on his feet, rage registering on his face. "What do you mean 'a tumor'? Are you saying that I'm not well? Are you telling us that after all that stinking chemotherapy, I still have cancer?"

"Hodgkin's is a tricky beast, Luke. Your lymph system networks your whole body. All it takes is one maverick cell to escape and settle elsewhere." The doctor's voice kept calm.

Nancy looked so pale, Julie thought she might faint, and Julie felt as if she herself might throw up. "I don't believe it. I don't believe that after all Luke's been through, he isn't cured of this thing," Julie cried.

"He's been in remission," the doctor said. "And when caught early, seventy-five percent of all newly diagnosed Hodgkin's *is* curable."

"But not Luke," Nancy said. "Not my son."

"This is a setback," Dr. Kessler conceded. "Usually remissions last longer."

"I don't want to go back on chemo," Luke shouted. "I don't want to take that stuff again."

Dr. Kessler stood and took Luke by the shoulders. "You won't do chemo again. At least, not now. I'm going to put you into radiation treatments."

"Radiation?" Nancy asked.

"Radiation will shrink the mass so that we can remove it surgically. It might possibly eliminate it altogether."

"I can't miss any more school." Luke sounded distraught. "I'm already behind and I don't want to be sick and throwing up like before."

"Radiation's not like chemo. And you won't have to come here to get the treatments. You can go to Waterton General. A friend of mine, Dr. John Laramore, is a radiation oncologist there, and he'll be handling your case."

Julie felt as if they were trapped in a bad dream, one that was circular and kept coming back to the same starting place. Why couldn't Luke get out of this nightmare?

Dr. Kessler made several phone calls and gave Luke fresh assurances. Then Julie, Luke, and his mother left and caught the train home. The very next day, Luke was to start his radiation therapy. He had planned to go to the gym and begin his weight-lifting schedule, but instead he would report to Dr. Laramore to begin another journey into the unknown.

Julie's father refused to believe the news when Julie told him. He ranted and raved, hopped into his car, and tore over to see Luke. Depressed and morose, Julie flopped on the sofa and flipped through the TV channels without pausing.

Her mother watched her for a few minutes, then came and took the remote control from her hand and turned the set off. She said, "I'm sorry, Julie."

"It isn't fair, Mom! Luke did exactly what the doctors told him to do—*everything!* And now he's right back at square one."

"Maybe not. Maybe the tumor is a freak thing that the radiation will clear right up."

"Well, I'm going with him tomorrow and I'm going to ask this new doctor a million questions."

"Julie . . . I—um . . ."

Julie looked up at her mother, who was chewing her bottom lip and looking perplexed. "What is it, Mom? What do you want to say to me? Don't tell me not to go. Because I *am* going."

Her mother sighed and sat down on the outermost edge of the sofa cushion, her hands folded neatly in her lap. "I wouldn't ask you not to go. I know how involved you've been in Luke's illness."

"So what's your point?"

"It's just that it *is* Luke's illness. You've gotten awfully wrapped up in this thing. Don't forget that you have a life to live too. You shouldn't let his health problems take over your whole existence."

"I can't believe you're saying this! You know how I feel about Luke. I can't abandon him."

"Don't be so dramatic. I'm not asking you to abandon him. I'm simply asking you to step back and get some perspective. You've gotten so wrapped up in this whole business that you've lost sight of your own goals and plans."

Fuming, Julie asked, "And what goals might those be?" How could her mother be so insensitive?

"You haven't done a single thing about college since our discussion last November. I'm telling you, Julie, now is the time to start applying. All the really top colleges fill up fast. If you aren't careful—"

Julie propelled herself off the couch. "I can't believe you're hounding me about something as unimportant as a college application! Don't you understand, Mom? Luke's cancer is back. He's not rid of it and . . . and . . ." Her voice began to waver.

"I didn't mean to upset you," her mother said in her most soothing tone. "I thought perhaps thinking about college would take your mind off Luke. Thinking about your future should be a fun thing."

Julie shook her head, and hot tears stung her eyes. "My future? You still don't get it, do you, Mother? Without Luke, I don't *have* a future. Without Luke, I don't even want one!"

She spun, ran from the room, and raced up the stairs, where she slammed her bedroom door hard behind her, then threw herself across her bed and sobbed.

As soon as school was out on Monday, Julie and Luke headed to Waterton's hospital, where Nancy joined them from her job at the mill. Dr. Laramore worked in an adjoining office building, on a floor named the Wilson Cancer Center. His suite was spacious and well decorated, with stacks of magazines, tables containing half-completed jigsaw puzzles, and, in the reception area, a desk that held a coffeemaker and ice-filled bowls with cartons of juice. "Help yourself," a nurse said. Luke declined.

Dr. Laramore was a pleasant-looking man, trim and well built, with a mustache. He ushered Luke, his mother, and Julie into his office and sat down at his desk. Julie took a deep breath, reached for Luke's hand, and thought, *Here we go again.*

"I've been over your records," the doctor said after introductions. "And I've studied your scans carefully. There's a growth in your chest and another, much smaller one in your groin."

Julie felt Luke's hand tighten around hers. "Dr. Kessler didn't mention that one."

"It wasn't as easy to detect. Besides, that's my job—to go over your scans with a magnifying glass." He paused, letting the news sink in.

"What will you do about it?" Nancy asked quietly.

"What we're going to do is bombard both areas with a mantle of radiation to damage these cancer cells and stop their growth. You'll be given a total of twenty treatments—five a week for a month. Nothing on the weekends."

Luke looked surprised. "That doesn't seem like much time. I mean compared with the chemo."

"You'll be receiving very high doses of radiation, and while it will be painless, there are side effects."

"Such as?"

"You'll be unusually tired. And the skin in the treated area will redden, as if you've gotten a mild sunburn. Apply no lotions or creams, though, unless I okay it. And because the treatments will be on your chest area, you may have a sore throat and difficulty swallowing . . . some loss of appetite is normal. You may develop a dry cough too."

Luke shook his head in disgust. "And the other area?" he asked.

Dr. Laramore steepled his fingers together and let his gaze bounce between Luke and Julie. "Often, both Hodgkin's and the treatments for Hodgkin's can cause fertility problems." He paused, waiting for their reactions.

"Are you saying my son might never have children?" Nancy's question brought the problem into sharp focus for Julie.

"It's a possibility. Although," he added quickly, "young men are more likely to regain their fertility than older men."

"Any other little tidbits?" Luke asked, his voice crisp, sarcastic. He did not look at Julie, but kept his eyes riveted on the doctor.

"That's about it." Dr. Laramore stood. "I'd like to get started as soon as possible. The first thing we'll do is define the exact area we're going to treat. We'll go back to one of the radiation rooms, where my technicians will measure, calculate, and mark you up. From the information, I'll create a graph to program the computer for your specific needs, taking into consideration your body density and the position of the tumors."

" 'Mark me up'?"

"With the help of lasers, we'll literally draw lines with a marking pen in a grid pattern on your body that I'll use to determine the exact spots that will receive the radiation. Try not to wash these lines off, because we'll use them every day."

"Can I shower?"

"Yes, but no soap on the marks until you've completed your treatments. The technicians will redraw the lines as they fade."

He walked them down the hall to a room where a large machine stood in the center of the floor, a bedlike table positioned under it. There were computers in the room and outside the door, which looked heavy and strong. "It's solid steel," one of the nurses said as Julie studied it. "Can't have any radiation leaking out."

Julie thought, *It'll be leaking into Luke's body*, but she didn't say it. Signs on the walls read: "Caution. X ray machines in use." She felt as if she'd stumbled into some sort of high-tech nuclear time warp. The machines looked cold and menacing.

"The two of you will have to wait in the lobby," a nurse told Julie and Nancy. "This will take about an hour."

"An hour?" Nancy sounded dismayed, and seemed hesitant to let her son remain inside the steel-lined room without her.

"The calculation part takes the longest,"

Dr. Laramore said kindly. "From now on, Luke will have a standing appointment to come in and be treated. The actual treatments take no more than a minute or so. And they're painless."

Julie and Luke's mother returned to the spacious lobby and took a seat. They didn't speak. Julie felt overwhelmed, imagining Luke being marked up like a piece of wild game after a kill. The doctors were going to shoot massive amounts of radiation into him in the hope of destroying the cancer cells that had invaded him. They were going to subject him to nuclear medical technology. And possibly rob him of his ability ever to have children.

"If it saves his life, it's a small price to pay," Nancy said quietly, as if she'd read Julie's mind. "His life is worth *any price.*"

12

"Are you sure it didn't hurt?" Julie asked Luke afterward when they returned to his house.

His mother had insisted Julie stay for dinner and was downstairs in the kitchen. Upstairs, in his room, the delicious aromas of browning hamburgers and sizzling onions permeated the air. Luke's bedroom was small, and the heavy oak furniture that had once belonged to his grandmother seemed too big for the space. Football trophies lined a shelf hung over his bed, while books had been stacked along a wall between his stereo and a study desk.

Large posters of a youthful Marilyn Monroe smiled beguilingly from his walls. Julie used to tease him about his "Marilyn fixation," but today she hardly noticed the pictures. She was apprehensive about his radiation therapy, and not hiding it.

"Didn't hurt a bit," Luke said. "I just had to lie really still while they drew on me." He lifted his shirt, and Julie saw bright blue lines on his skin that disappeared below the waistband of his jeans. "Actually, it sort of tickled."

She leaned in closer, squinting. "What are those little dots between the blue lines?" She followed the small dots down his chest with her eyes.

"Tattoos," he said. "Permanent marks so that the technician can always line up the machine perfectly. If the radiation beam is even a tiny degree off, the wrong part of my body will get the radiation."

"So they play connect-the-dots on your skin every time?"

"That's right." He pulled his shirt down to cover the blue lines. "Personally, if I got a tattoo, I'd have picked something more exciting—like a mermaid, or a heart." He patted his upper arm. "It would read 'Luke loves Julie.' "

She appreciated his trying to lighten her mood, but she didn't like this radiation business one bit. "I want to go with you for your treatments. What time's your next appointment?"

"Every day at three-thirty, but I don't want you to come."

"But why?" His response surprised her.

"I've been thinking about it, Julie, and there's nothing for you to do but sit in the lobby. I'd rather go on in by myself, get my treatment, then head to the gym."

"The gym? But the doctor said you'd be tired."

"I don't care what the doctor said. So long as I'm able to function, I'm going to stick with my normal routine."

"But there's all that juice to drink and all those puzzles to work at the radiation center." She hoped humor would persuade him to let her come along.

"Sitting around waiting is boring, Julie. I don't want you to do it anymore."

"But—"

"Please," he interrupted. "It's what I want."

She was frustrated, but she didn't argue.

Every afternoon that week, Luke left school as soon as classes were dismissed. He didn't change his mind about Julie accompanying him to the cancer center; in fact, he kept to himself even at school, telling Julie that he didn't have much of an appetite and that he was skipping lunch. And in the evenings, he told her he was cramming for finals and thought it best he do it alone.

On Friday, he insisted he was tired and wanted to turn in early and that she should make other plans. Confused by his behavior, but determined not to let it dishearten her, Julie invited Solena to spend the night.

"I don't get it," Julie told her friend as they sat on her bedroom floor, sorting through old photos and nibbling on popcorn. "Why is he shutting me out this way?"

"It *is* kind of a mystery," Solena agreed. "I mean, the whole time Luke was in the hospital and even when he went through chemo, he wanted you with him. Frankly, I can't see the difference between radiation and the other."

"Me either. I don't understand him these days. He's so moody. I can't figure out what he wants from me."

"Did you do something to make him angry?"

"Like what?"

"Like flirt with another guy."

Julie rolled her eyes in exasperation. "Grow up, Solena. I haven't *thought* about anybody but Luke since he got sick. And even before that, I didn't want to date anybody else."

"Sorry . . . I lost my head. I know you and Luke are number one with each other." Solena grew silent, contemplative. Finally, she said, "You know, what's happened to Luke has brought Frank and me closer."

"How so?"

"If something like cancer could happen to a guy like Luke, it could happen to any of us."

"Nobody gets to pick what life gives them," Julie said, toying with a photo of her and Luke from their ninth-grade dance. They both looked so young. And so happy. She sighed and tossed the photo aside.

"Frank's gotten a little paranoid," Solena continued. "Every time he feels a bump or lump, or even if he has a headache, he gets squirrelly. He says, 'Solena, look at this. Do you think it's anything serious?' As if I'd know."

"He can't live his whole life thinking he's going to get some dread disease."

"That's what I tell him, but he still worries. He's always popping vitamins and eating health foods—as if that will keep him from ever getting sick."

"It can't hurt. Luke's doctors have said that

his good physical condition helped him recover so quickly from chemo and the biopsies. And I know he's working hard to get his fitness back so he can play ball next year."

Solena began absently to arrange kernels of popcorn in a straight line on the carpet. "Can I ask you something?"

"Ask."

"Did you and Luke ever talk about getting married someday?"

"He asked me to marry him in the sixth grade."

Solena made a face at Julie. "I meant sometime more recent."

Julie wasn't sure how to answer. Sure, she'd been secretly planning to attend whatever college Luke chose, but she knew he wanted a shot at a career in professional football, and she wasn't sure whether marriage and pro ball would mix. "You know my mother would croak if I got married before I climb some corporate ladder."

"But do you want to marry Luke? Would you if he asked you?"

Unwilling to answer, Julie decided to go on the offensive. "You must be curious for a reason. Are you and Frank thinking about marriage?"

"Not exactly, but he's been awfully nice to me lately."

"You're usually worried about him dumping you and dating someone else."

"I told you this whole business with Luke has changed him."

"Seems like a good change to me."

"In some ways it is. But in some ways it's scary." Julie looked quizzical, and Solena hastened to explain. "It's like he suddenly got old. Like life is serious business and he shouldn't have fun anymore. As if having too much fun is something taboo."

As Solena struggled to express her thoughts, Julie nodded. "You mean, if his best friend has to suffer then he should too."

"Yes!" Solena cried. "That's exactly what I mean. He feels guilty because he's healthy and Luke isn't."

"Luke's going to get well."

"I know he is," Solena said. Yet her tone wasn't as convincing as her statement.

"And when he does then everything will be like it used to be. And everybody will act like they used to act."

"You think so?"

"Absolutely." Julie waved her hand and scattered the line of popcorn Solena had so carefully arranged. "Hey, let's say we sneak downstairs and watch a movie. My folks should be dead to the world by now."

"Good idea." Solena rose and scooped up the bowl of popcorn. She paused, saying, "I'm glad we talked, Julie. I didn't have anybody else to tell about Frank, and I knew you'd understand."

"Once Luke recovers, Frank will be his old self. Wait and see."

"One more thing," Solena added. "I'm glad you invited me over tonight. I've missed you. I know how involved you've been with Luke and that's okay, but still, I miss the stuff we used to do together. Not just you and me, but you and Luke and Frank and me. We sure had some good times."

"I've missed the old days too."

Solena sighed and shrugged. "Oh, well, I don't mean to be a party pooper, but I did want you to know how I feel."

"Thanks." Julie gave her friend a quick hug.

They pattered down the stairs and into the family room, popped a tape into the VCR, and settled down to watch. But Julie could hardly follow the story line because her mind kept wandering back to Luke. The cool way he was treating her had her mystified—and worried. She didn't understand why he wasn't letting her remain close to him. Or why he insisted on going through his latest series of treatments by himself. It wasn't like Luke. He *always* wanted her with him.

The next day she casually asked her father how he thought Luke was behaving.

"Like he wants to put this whole mess behind him and get on with his life," her father told her with a pleased smile. "He's working hard in the gym. I'm impressed at the way he's making a comeback."

"Well, maybe he should be taking it easier."

"Aw, Julie-girl, don't go trying to turn Luke into a wimp. He's doing just fine. No need to hover over him like some kind of watchdog."

"Really, Dad, that's not what I'm doing. I'm just questioning if he's overdoing it or not."

"No way," her father said with a wave of dismissal, but Julie wasn't so sure. She also didn't know whether Luke's new attitude came from a genuine desire to refocus his attention onto football or from a desire to back away from her. But she was determined to figure it out.

13

Luke was halfway through his radiation treatments when school let out for the summer. On the last day of classes, Julie found him down at the construction site of the new stadium. Bulldozers were moving dirt and the rickety old bleachers had been partially torn down to make way for the new. "Hi," she called over the noise of the big yellow machines.

"Hi yourself."

"Looks like real progress, doesn't it?"

"It's going to be a great stadium."

She gazed up at him longingly, wishing he'd take her in his arms the way he used to do. She recalled her vow to figure out what had gone wrong between them and realized that she was more perplexed than ever. Luke rarely asked her out these days, keeping to himself, shunning contact with almost everybody. "So, what's on your agenda for your first week of summer vacation?" she asked brightly, hoping to draw him into conversation.

"I'm doubling my efforts in the gym."

"Can you do that?" She thought he looked tired.

"Dr. Laramore says I can do whatever I feel like doing, and I want to get back into shape as quick as I can." He sounded cross with her for even asking.

They listened to the roar of the machines while Julie racked her brain for another topic. "I start my job at the library Monday."

"I hope you like it."

If this had been a normal summer, he'd be taking her to the library and making plans to pick her up afterward. If they'd been spending their spare time together, she wouldn't feel so awkward around him. They'd be talking all the time and would know what was going on in each other's lives. "Once the radiation's over, what will you do?"

"I'll have to go into Chicago for a day or so of testing."

"Do you want me to come with you?" she asked anxiously, hoping he'd say yes.

"No. It's not a big deal. Just all those boring tests and scans again."

"I don't mind."

"Forget it. Mom and I'll trudge through it."

Again, the roar of a bulldozer broke into their conversation. Julie felt grateful for the interruption. His rejection stung, and she didn't trust her voice. "And then?" she asked when the noise died down and she'd regained her composure. "Do you think you'll take a summer job?" He had always worked summers to help out his mother.

"Who's going to hire someone like me? I could get sick again."

He sounded bitter, and she felt sorry for him. "So you won't do anything?"

"Remember me telling you about Los Angeles?" She nodded. "Uncle Steve called and said he'll send me a plane ticket the minute I agree to come."

"So you're going?"

"I'm going."

"How long will you stay?"

"About a month. I'll be home in time for August practice."

"Of course." Her stomach knotted. She remembered telling him to take the vacation, and after all he'd been through he deserved to go somewhere and have fun. But she knew she'd miss him terribly, and that it wouldn't be easy seeing him leave when she wanted to be with him so much. "I hope you have a good time in L.A. Do you still want me to write you?"

"If you'd like . . . but I won't be leaving until July."

Julie decided to try one more time to lure him out of his shell. "How about us doing something with each other tonight? Solena's having a party to celebrate the end of the school year. Why don't you take me?"

"Um—I don't think I feel up to it. You go on without me."

"But you feel good enough to go to the gym this afternoon?"

She'd tripped him up, and his face flushed red. "Julie . . . I never know exactly how I'm going to feel. . . ."

"No problem," she said, backing away. "I'll go without you."

"Julie, I—" He looked troubled, but she brushed it aside, suddenly wanting to get as far away as possible from the noise of the machinery and the pain Luke was causing her.

"I've got to go." She turned and darted off.

"You'll let me know about your first day of work?" he called as she fled.

She felt like saying, *Fat chance!* But she didn't. Because no matter how badly he was hurting her, she knew she couldn't hurt him. She couldn't because she loved him. She couldn't because something deep inside her kept saying that he still loved her too. And it was that ray of hope that she clung to.

The golden sunshine of Monday morning did little to dispel Julie's gloom. The weekend had been long and difficult. She'd reached for the phone many times to call Luke, but each time she'd pulled back, telling herself that if he wanted to talk to her, he would call. Except that he hadn't.

She left for her new job at the library, entered the hushed building, went to Mrs. Watson's office, and knocked on the closed door. She was ushered inside by a heavyset woman with graying hair and lavender-framed eyeglasses.

"Julie! So glad you'll be working with us this summer," Mrs. Watson said with a smile as she pumped Julie's hand.

" 'Us'?"

"Yes. Meet my nephew, Jason Lawrence."

She gestured to a tall, slim boy with blond hair and green eyes. "Jason's a sophomore at Ball State University in Muncie and he'll be living with me this summer, and working here too."

"Hello, Julie Ellis," Jason said with a grin that sent her a message of approval.

She smiled politely, but coolly.

Mrs. Watson went on to discuss their respective duties. The work seemed simple enough to Julie, and by lunchtime she had begun to catalog a stack of new volumes while Jason manned the front checkout desk. He asked her to lunch, but she told him no. By the end of the workday, Julie could barely keep from dashing out the door. "Take you home?" Jason asked as she hurried past. "Maybe you could show me around town."

"Can't tonight," she told him. All the way home, she pondered her situation. Julie had gotten a plum of a job without any effort. She was working with a good-looking college boy who was going to be around all summer. She was to be working with him all day, every day, for three solid months.

Grimly, Julie pulled into her driveway and hurried into her house. Her situation looked like a setup. And it had her mother's fingerprints all over it.

She found her mother in the den, sorting through piles of papers. "How was your first day?" Patricia Ellis asked cheerfully.

"Did you know Mrs. Watson's nephew is working at the library too?" Julie asked without preamble.

Her mother's gaze avoided Julie's. "I think she mentioned it to me. Is he nice?"

"I think he wants to date me," Julie said boldly.

"Well, that might be fun. I'm sure he'd like to make friends—"

"Mother!" Julie interrupted. "How could you? Did you think I was going to fall into some other guy's arms just because we were working together every day?"

Her mother looked startled. "I don't know what you mean."

"You don't let me drive to the mall without a third degree and yet when I told you some stranger you've never met wants to date me—which, incidentally, I made up—you say, 'That might be fun.' "

Color stained her mother's face. "Well, of course, I'd have expected you to bring the boy to meet your dad and me. What do you mean, you 'made it up'?"

"I mean that I'm not interested in anybody

but Luke. No one is going to come along and make me forget him."

"I never expected you to stop dating Luke, but I have noticed how things have cooled off between the two of you, and when Mrs. Watson told me about her nephew and about how he's a journalism major at Ball State, I thought that maybe you'd like to get to know him. He can tell you a lot about college life, Julie. Ball State is a fine school, one you should apply to this summer."

"I don't believe this." Julie felt furious. "I don't believe you're trying to sabotage my life."

"Oh, really—"

"No, it's true. Please hear me, Mother, once and for all. I don't want to date anyone else but Luke. I *will* go to college and I *will* start applying in the fall. But this is summer vacation and Luke is sick and he needs me."

"He certainly hasn't acted much like it," her mother fired back. "You sit home most of the time waiting for him to call."

"Well, that's about to change," Julie said. She grabbed her purse from her mother's desk and fished out her keys. "I'm going to Luke's. Don't wait supper for me."

"Julie!" Her mother called.

But Julie wasn't listening. She rushed out the door, jumped into her car, and sped across town to Luke's house. She pounded on the door until he opened it. He looked shocked at seeing her. "What's wrong?"

"That's what *I'd* like to know, Luke." Julie brushed past him and planted herself in the center of his living room floor. She crossed her arms and leveled her gaze at him.

"Nothing's wrong," he insisted.

"Guess again."

"I don't know what you want me to say."

She rolled her eyes in exasperation. "You sound like my mother."

"What do you mean?"

"Never mind." She glared at him. "You've been ignoring me for weeks, Luke."

"No," he said quickly. "I've just been giving you space."

"Space for what?"

"*Space.* You know, breathing room."

"Did I ask you for breathing room?"

He raked his fingers through his hair, which had grown to over an inch. "I don't want to fight with you, Julie."

"Good, because I don't want to fight with you either." She took a deep breath and held it. Finally, she said, "My new job is going to work out fine. There's a college guy working with me who's really nice. He wants me to go out with him."

"Are you?"

"I'm considering it."

A flood of emotions crossed Luke's face. "Please don't." His voice was scarcely a whisper.

"Why shouldn't I? I mean, you're giving me all this *space.* I can't sit around doing nothing with it."

He came to her in one long stride, threw his arms around her, and crushed her against his body. "Don't, Julie," he pleaded, sounding tortured. "Don't leave me. I can't make it without you."

14

After the way he'd been acting toward her during the past weeks, Julie was caught off guard by his impassioned plea. She said, "You *have* been avoiding me, Luke. And it hurts." Tears welled in her eyes. Her anger was gone, but not her frustration.

Slowly, Luke released her. He took her hand and walked her to the sofa, where he sat her down and studied her face with his dark brown eyes, so intently that she thought she might drown in them. "Staying away from you hasn't been easy for me."

"Why would you do it in the first place? If you're miserable and I'm miserable, why would you continue to ignore me?"

"That's not what I was trying to do, Julie." He sat next to her without releasing her hand.

"I—I really don't know how to explain what I've been feeling."

"Try."

"It really bummed me out when the cancer flared up again and I had to start radiation. After I went through chemo, I thought it was finished. Instead, I discovered it had just begun. Dumb of me."

"But this could be a fluke. Once you complete radiation, it'll be gone for good. You've done it all—chemo and radiation. What's left?"

"If this doesn't do the trick," he said quietly, "I'll need a bone marrow transplant. If the cancer spreads to my bone marrow, there's no other treatment."

A chill frosted her heart and made her stomach tighten. She'd read enough and seen enough on TV to know that bone marrow donors were scarce, mostly because it was so difficult to find a compatible match. "You aren't there yet," she said emphatically. "And I don't think you ever will be. Chemo and radiation will do the trick. You'll see."

"A lot will depend on how the tests turn out in Chicago. The scans and bone marrow aspiration will tell the story."

"I know." She squeezed his hand. "And

speaking of the hospital, why won't you let me come with you? Why are you shutting me out?"

"Maybe because I'm worried the scans won't be all right."

"Don't you want me with you if the news is bad?"

He looked vulnerable and terrified. "Yes. More than anything."

"Then let me come."

"I want you to have a regular life, Julie. You shouldn't have to sit around hospitals and doctors' offices waiting for me. Waiting to see if my life's going down the toilet or not."

"Luke, tell me, what's a 'regular life'? Dating someone else?"

He answered her question with one of his own. "Do you like this guy from the library? Do you really want to date him?"

"No way. But *you're* not dating me either."

"It's because I hate tying you down." He glanced at the floor, looking ashamed. "If I love you, I should want what's best for you, and you didn't sign up for having a sick boyfriend. You're beautiful, Julie, and you should have more than I'm giving you. You should be going to parties and doing stuff that's fun."

Her heart went out to him as the reason for

his actions became clearer to her. "So you thought by avoiding me, I'd get interested in somebody else."

"Yes."

"But when I told you I might date somebody else—"

"I couldn't stand it," he blurted. "I love you so much it hurts. So you see, I'm not only sick, I'm a coward too."

She eased off the couch, knelt on the floor in front of him, rested her palms on his thighs, and gazed into his face. "I hate what's happening to you, Luke. I think it's gross and unfair and horrible. But it doesn't change the way I feel about you. I still love you, and the feeling isn't going away."

The look he gave her reminded her of a drowning man miraculously thrown a lifeline. He caressed her cheek gently and she turned her head and kissed the inside of his palm. "I'm sorry, Julie. Sorry if I hurt you in any way. I only want what's best for you, and sitting around waiting for me to get well doesn't seem like something you should have to do."

"But it's what I *want* to do. And this time next year, when this is all over, being with you is still where I'll want to be. This time next year, you'll have a college all picked out, and wherever you go, I'll go."

"But your mother—"

"Will live with it. I figure you'll only take a scholarship to a great college, so she'll be happy when I choose the same great college. No matter how you look at it, everybody wins."

"*If* I get offered a scholarship." Luke's face clouded. "Who'll want me, Julie? What college coach is going to take a chance on a quarterback who has cancer?"

"You'll be well by then. And remember, my father's on your side. He won't allow anybody to reject you because of possible health problems."

"You have more faith than I do."

She patted his hand and rose. "One of us has to."

He stood and took her by the shoulders. "When I go for my testing in two weeks, will you come with me?"

"Absolutely," she said with satisfaction.

"And this guy at the library who wants to date you?"

"Is history."

A slow smile spread over Luke's face, making Julie's knees go weak and her pulse flutter.

"Let's go to a movie, and afterward get ice cream to celebrate," he said.

"I'd love to. I missed dinner tonight."

"Then I owe you," he said. "I owe you big time." Luke swept her into his arms and buried her mouth in a kiss.

Julie, Luke, and his mother made the trip to Chicago one warm morning during the last week of June. Julie held Luke's hand while he stared pensively out the train window. She knew he was worried. The last time they'd made the trip they'd expected everything to be fine, but things hadn't been fine. And now, after weeks of radiation, Luke had no assurances that he was rid of his cancer.

At the hospital, Julie and Nancy followed Luke from department to department throughout the long day of testing. They sat in cubicles and lounges, flipped through magazines, watched dull afternoon TV. The three of them ate lunch in the hospital cafeteria amid the clank and clatter of trays and silverware. No one ate much.

In the late afternoon, Dr. Kessler ushered them into his office. Julie's palms were sweating and she felt sick to her stomach, remembering the last time he'd spoken to them and dropped the bomb about the tumor. But today, he was all smiles.

"You're looking good, Luke."

"Really?"

"Thank God," Nancy whispered, her voice trembling.

The CT and bone scan films were spread across the light board hanging on the wall behind his desk. "We won't have the results of the bone marrow aspiration for a few days, but I don't expect any surprises."

Luke rubbed his hip, which was still sore from where the needle had been inserted to extract marrow for the test. "So I'm cured?"

"I didn't say that."

Julie's elation did a stutter-step. "But if there aren't any bad cells? . . ." she began.

"I prefer to think of your disease as in remission," Dr. Kessler explained. "No two cases of cancer are alike, but the longer you remain in remission, the higher the probability that you'll recover completely."

A grin split Luke's face. "I don't care what you call it, I just want to be rid of it."

"What do we do now?" his mother asked.

"Go home and have a great summer. I'll see you in three months."

Luke fairly sprang out of his chair. "Let's

get out of here," he said to Julie and his mother.

After good-byes to the doctor and staff and the scheduling of another testing day in September, they headed for the train station. This time, the ride back passed in a state of euphoria. This time, even though dusk was falling, the world zipping by the window looked bright and beautiful.

Once home, they decided against a party. But Julie's father insisted on celebrating and took all of them out to dinner at a fancy restaurant on the outskirts of Chicago.

The dinner was perfect and her father couldn't stop grinning and slapping Luke on the back and toasting him with pitchers of iced tea. Julie's mother seemed equally happy over the news and Luke's mother couldn't take her eyes off her son.

"I knew you'd lick this thing," Coach Ellis kept saying. "Can't keep a good man down for long."

Under the table, Luke slipped his hand into Julie's, and when they returned to Waterton that night, he gave her six long-stemmed red roses—one for every week he'd isolated himself from her. She put them in a vase and fingered the petals tenderly. "You always can get to me with flowers, Luke Muldenhower. They're beautiful."

"So are you."

"I'm going to miss you when you go off to Los Angeles," she confessed.

"I want to talk to you about that."

She noticed that his eyes were glowing and realized he'd been guarding a secret. "What about it?"

"I called my uncle and told him that as much as I appreciated his offer, I couldn't come."

"No, Luke—"

"Just listen. I told him that I couldn't stand to be away from you, not even for a free month in California."

She shook her head, thrilled in one way, sorry in another. "You call him back and tell him you're coming."

"Well, that's just it." Luke brushed her long blond hair off her bare shoulders. "He called me last night and said that if you were that important to me, then he'd send you a ticket also."

Her mouth dropped open. "You mean he wants us to come together?"

"And to stay at his condo and to show us the time of our lives." His face clouded momentarily. "Do you think you can come, Julie? I know you have a job and all, but if you can't come with me I don't want to go."

She nibbled at her bottom lip, contemplating the situation. "The job's nothing. Solena can take it over."

"But your parents . . . what will they say?"

More than anything, Julie wanted to go with Luke. She wanted to spend as much time as possible with him. The need to do so felt compelling and urgent. She couldn't be separated from him, not even for a month. Steely resolve stole through her. "I'm going, Luke," she said. "And don't worry, I'll persuade my parents."

"But your mother—"

"Leave my mother to me . . . I'll handle her. I promise." Julie was thinking about the way her mother had manipulated the job so that Julie could spend time with the librarian's nephew. "Believe me, Mom owes me this one," Julie added. She slipped into Luke's arms and sealed her vow to him with a kiss.

15

The plane descended through a bank of thick white clouds tinged in pink, and aimed for the long runway of Los Angeles International Airport. Julie pressed her nose to the small, oblong window, peering down at the cityscape spread out below. She clutched Luke's arm. "My gosh, look. There's civilization as far as I can see."

Luke craned his neck to peer past her shoulder. "It's sure nothing like Indiana. And look at the expressways!" Superhighways looped like broad, flat ribbons through the concrete maze of buildings. In the far distance, foothills, looking brown and parched, rolled across arid stretches of ground.

They had left Chicago's O'Hare Airport at 7 A.M. and chased the rising sun westward. Because of the time change, the plane would land close to the time it had departed Chicago. "How will you know your uncle?" Julie asked.

Luke extracted a photograph from the pocket of his shirt. "He sent Mom this last Christmas." A tall man with brown hair, broad shoulders, and a winning smile stood beside a petite red-haired woman. Both were wearing hiking gear. "And of course, he has a picture of me."

Once the plane landed, Luke grabbed up his backpack and Julie her satchel, and they deplaned, walked through a doorway, and found themselves in a throng of people. Julie caught her breath. She'd never seen such crowds.

"Luke! Over here!"

Julie and Luke turned to see a man waving from his position beside a round white pillar. A red-haired woman, who looked to be in her thirties, held his other hand. After hugs, Luke introduced Julie and Uncle Steve introduced the woman as Diedra O'Ryan, his "significant other."

Steve insisted on first names and Julie liked the idea. She felt awkward calling him "Uncle" when he wasn't kin to her. "Trip okay?" Steve asked.

"Perfect," Luke said.

Steve studied him. "You look so much like my brother."

"Mom's showed me photos of Dad, but I don't see the resemblance," Luke replied.

"Trust me," Steve said, still studying Luke's face. "You're the image of him at seventeen. It's like seeing a ghost."

"Are you tired?" Diedra asked, interrupting the bittersweet reminiscing.

"Not really. We got up at four to catch the limo bus to O'Hare," Julie answered quickly. "But I've been so excited about the trip that I hadn't slept all night anyway."

"I'm glad your parents let you come," Steve told her.

"After you called and talked to them, and after Luke's mother assured them that I'd be safe with you in L.A., and after I whimpered and whined for a week, they had no choice," Julie declared with a satisfied smile.

They laughed. Julie didn't add how tough the sell had been or how she'd brazenly pitted her parents against one another to get her way. In the end, her father had come over to her side, and although her mother hadn't been happy, she had resigned herself to Julie's making the trip.

"We've got a ton of things planned to do while you're here," Steve said.

"We want to do it *all,*" Julie said.

By now they'd entered the baggage claim area, and Steve and Luke went to retrieve his and Julie's luggage. Diedra asked, "How's Luke feeling?"

"Really good. Planning this trip was fun and gave him lots to think about besides cancer."

Diedra nodded. "Steve's been worried sick ever since he found out. We would have come to Indiana, but Steve didn't want Luke to think that the family had been called in for a bedside vigil."

"Luke wouldn't have wanted Steve to see him following chemo anyway. He lost all his hair and got really ill. And then the radiation made him so tired, he wouldn't have wanted his uncle to visit then either."

"Steve figured a vacation in L.A. would be much more healthy than a race to Luke's bedside."

"Good choice. Luke's over the worst of it now, and this is the way he wants his uncle to see him—not sick with cancer."

"I understand." Diedra's green eyes

clouded. "My mother died from cancer five years ago. It was hard watching her suffer."

Julie tossed her long blond hair. "Well, that's not going to happen to Luke. His last checkup was perfect, and now all he wants is to get on with his life."

"And with you cheering him on, I'm sure his life will be interesting." Diedra's eyes sparkled mischievously, and Julie blushed. "I told Steve that the time to go east for a visit is when Luke's healthy and playing football again."

Julie nodded. "Good idea. With Luke, our high school has a great shot at going to the playoffs. At least that's what my father says."

"You make Luke sound like a true hero."

"Okay, so I'm his biggest fan."

"Good for you." Julie's gaze connected with Diedra's, and she knew she had made a friend.

The ride to Steve's condo community took them down expressways with names on exit ramps that Julie had only read about or seen in movies and music videos. At one point, high on a hill, she saw the tall white letters of "Hollywood" spelled out. Steve promised them a day of touring the famous area.

Steve's neighborhood contained rows of town houses that looked alike—white stucco walls, red barrel-tile roofs, and red-painted doors. Some homes had wrought-iron grill-work over windows and Spanish-tile walk-ways. Clumps of hibiscus bushes and vines of bright fuchsia bougainvillea lined medians and gateways.

Steve's three-story town house was spacious, built so that all the downstairs rooms looked out onto an inner courtyard with a tiled garden and a bubbling fountain. "Beautiful," Julie cried.

Upstairs, Julie's and Luke's room each had its own bathroom. "I saw a place like this once in a magazine," Julie told Luke when they were alone. "What's your uncle do for a job, anyway?"

"He's a cinematographer. Far cry from the steel mills, don't you think?"

Julie recalled the cornfields of her home area, the towering grain silos, the smoke-belching stacks of the mills. "It's different, all right. Maybe some college out here will want you."

Luke shrugged. "This is a long way from Indiana."

"Thanks for bringing me, Luke."

He pulled her into his arms. "I couldn't have come without you."

Diedra called to them from the bottom of the stairs. "You two want some chow?"

In response, Luke's stomach growled, sending Julie into a fit of laughter. They bolted down the stairs and Diedra took them through sliding glass doors and into the courtyard, where a table set with platters of fresh fruit and sandwiches stood waiting. Steve was on a portable phone, but he signaled them to sit down. Julie sat facing the fountain, a large concrete pedestal holding a boy riding a dolphin, studded with colorful tile. Water bubbled into a basin where lily pads and pale pink lotus flowers floated. Sunlight dazzled Julie's eyes and flecked off the dancing water.

"Do you want to rest?" Steve asked as soon as he was off the phone.

"No way," Luke said, biting into a thick sandwich. "I spent months resting. All I want to do now is *go*." He paused. "But what about your work?" At the mills back home everyone worked shifts.

"I'm taking some time off," Steve said. "I've earned it. And besides, how often does my brother's kid come to visit me?"

"What about you, Diedra?"

"I work with Steve," she said. "We have a

two-month hiatus before we start our next film. So, I'm coming along for the fun."

Julie was glad. And very impressed by Steve and Diedra's glamorous profession. All at once, she began to get a glimmer of what her mother kept harping about when she said that the world was a big place and that Julie owed it to herself to check it out. Still, for right now, her world was high school. And Luke. Always Luke. She couldn't forget that. But perhaps, together, the two of them could discover the rest of the world and find a place in it for themselves, the way Steve and Diedra had.

"So what would you like to see first?" Steve wanted to know.

"Hollywood," Luke said without hesitation.

"And that sidewalk with all the movie stars' handprints," Julie added.

Steve grinned. "I figured you'd want to go there, so that'll be our first stop. I've made reservations for dinner at Planet Hollywood . . . unless you'd rather go to the Hard Rock Cafe."

"Let's go to both," Luke said quickly, making them laugh.

"You do have a whole month out here," Diedra teased.

"We'll go to Universal Studios, Disneyland, visit a movie production set, take a hike up in the hills—"

"How about Rodeo Drive?" Julie blurted out the name of the most famous shopping area in Beverly Hills. "I promised Solena I'd buy her something from there."

"What?" Luke asked. "A pack of chewing gum? That place is expensive."

"I know a few stores we can shop at," Diedra assured them. She glanced at Steve, who cleared his throat.

"But before we take off, there is something very special I want you to plan on doing with me and Diedra while you're here."

"Name it." Luke tilted his head, his expression curious.

"It's a big favor," Steve said. "And we need both of you to help."

"Count me in," Julie said, also curious as to what she could possibly do for them.

Steve reached over and laced his large fingers through Diedra's small, delicate ones. "While you're here, Diedra and I want to get married. And we want you two to be our best man and maid of honor. What do you say?"

16

"**M**arried?" Luke's face broke into a grin. "That's cool. You bet I'll be your best man."

Julie felt less enthusiastic. She'd only just met them and didn't feel qualified to be a maid of honor. "But what about your family? And how about your best friends? Won't any of them want to be in your wedding?" Personally, she couldn't imagine getting married without Solena standing with her.

"I'm the only one left in my family," Diedra said. "And Steve's my best friend." She patted his hand affectionately. "And we made up our mind that we want the wedding to be very small and very intimate. We just want the two of you there."

"And I was the best man at your parents' wedding," Steve said. "If my brother were still alive, I'd ask him, but you're his son and that's the next best thing to his being there."

"When are we going to do this?" Luke wanted to know.

"We were thinking about the week right before you go home. There's this little chapel up the coast and that's were we want to do the deed."

"The chapel's beautiful," Diedra added. "And quite old. The Spanish settlers built it in the 1700s and monks still take care of the place."

By now, Julie too was caught up in the excitement. It all seemed so romantic. "I didn't bring anything very dressy."

"Rodeo Drive, remember? My treat," Diedra said with a wink.

Steve groaned. "Dress shopping?" He glanced at Luke. "While they shop, we'll knock some golf balls around."

"Suits me," Luke said.

After more discussion, more food, and two quick phone calls to Indiana so that Luke and Julie could tell their parents they'd arrived safely, the four of them headed for Hollywood. On the way to the car, Luke plucked a bright red hibiscus flower and tucked it behind Julie's ear.

"Pretty," he said gazing into her eyes, and she caught the double implication of his compliment.

Hollywood's Walk of Fame was a long sidewalk teeming with tourists, where star shapes had been set in granite and concrete, each bearing the name of some famous screen personage. At Grauman's Chinese Theater, signatures were scrawled in the cement, accompanied by handprints. Julie and Luke shouldered their way through throngs of tourists, exclaiming over names they recognized, pausing to ask about names they didn't. Steve knew a great deal about the silver screen and kept up a running commentary. "He's better than a tour guide," Diedra confided.

The names rolled past Julie's vision, and sometimes she hesitated even to step on a particular slab, as if it might desecrate the person's memory. The sun beat down on her back and shoulders, but she was so immersed in stargazing that she barely felt its heat. All of a sudden, Luke stopped and pointed down.

There in the concrete was the signature of Marilyn Monroe, her handprints above her name. He whipped off his baseball cap and placed it over his heart. "A moment of reverence, please."

"You an MM fan?" Steve asked.

"She's the other woman in his life," Julie explained. "But I've learned to live with it."

Luke paced around the square bearing Marilyn's name and handprints. Tourists streamed by them, snapping pictures and exclaiming over other names. "You know what, Julie? I'll bet your hands are the same size."

"I'll bet not."

"Only one way to find out."

She glanced at all the foot traffic. "I'll get stepped on."

"We'll protect you," Steve said. He and Diedra and Luke formed a circle around her.

"Are you kidding?" But a glance at their faces told her they weren't.

"Come on," Luke urged. "What can it hurt? Don't you want to know?"

She sighed, dropped to her knees on the hot concrete, and carefully placed her hands into the mold of Marilyn's. To her astonishment, it was a perfect fit. "I don't believe it."

Luke whooped and his face split into a grin. "I knew it! I knew your hands would be the same size. This is so cool."

Julie stood. "That's about all of me that's the same size."

Luke seized her around the waist and lifted

her off the ground, laughing. "I have a living duplicate of Marilyn. Does life get much better than this?"

Julie blushed furiously. He was causing a scene and a small crowd was looking on with curiosity. "He's crazy," she mouthed apologetically to the onlookers. "Heat stroke."

Luke bent her backward and kissed her soundly on the mouth. The crowd broke into applause.

"Luke! This is *so* embarrassing," Julie hissed.

"So what? We'll never see these people again. Besides, life is short."

Steve and Diedra stood to one side and laughed. When Julie was finally able to regain her composure, they headed off to other attractions. She pretended to be in a huff, but of course she wasn't. If anything, she was more in love with Luke than ever. Not because he'd kissed her in public, but because he wasn't afraid to show his feelings for her to the whole world.

Yet his statement, "Life is short," haunted her the rest of the day. She'd heard the phrase many times, but when Luke said it, it took on a deeper, more profound meaning. *Life was short.* And only a person who had looked death in the face could understand how very short it really could be.

The days passed in a whirlwind of activity and blended into one another like colors flowing across the sky at sunset. Julie fell in love with California. Steve took them on some great driving tours. Julie thought the city of Los Angeles too large, too busy, too filled with smog and exhaust fumes. But in the valleys, where farmers grew lush green crops, and in the foothills, where cactus and jagged rock formations looked wild and untamed, and on the beaches, where ocean waves rolled in timeless swirls, she lost her heart. And because she could share it all with Luke, the beauty and grandeur of the state took on an almost hallowed meaning for her.

"Promise me you'll bring me back here someday," she said to him one starry night when they were alone by Steve's courtyard fountain.

"You mean leave Indiana?" His eyes danced mischievously.

"I could be persuaded." She dipped her hand into the cool water, where golden fish swam lazily beneath lily pads.

"But remember the smell of autumn—of

woodsmoke, and how the leaves change colors. Can you leave all that for this?"

Memories of chilly nights and football games and the thrill of the year's first snowfall came to her. She felt a twinge of homesickness. "But don't forget there aren't any flowers half the year. And you know how much I like flowers."

"Well, I like it here too." His voice sounded low and soft in the velvet night. "It's hard to think about going home."

"Then don't think about it. We've got two more weeks."

He leaned back against the bowl of the fountain, rested his elbows on the lip, and gazed up at the glittering stars. "Sometimes, the past six months seem like a bad dream. Like they never happened to me. I wish I didn't have to go for testing ever again."

A chill coursed through her as the memories flooded back. "The testing's routine. The results were fine last time and they'll be fine next time too. I'm telling you, Luke, it's over. You've licked Hodgkin's." Suddenly, a new fear seized her, and she leaned toward him. "You are feeling all right, aren't you?"

"Me? I feel great. I'm sorry, I didn't mean

to alarm you. I was just thinking out loud, that's all."

She sighed with relief. "Good. We've been so busy and you've seemed so energetic—what with working out every day—that sometimes I forget . . . you know . . . about your health."

"I forget about it too." He stood and drew her up into his arms. "And I didn't mean to bring you down by talking about it."

"No problem." She rested her head on his broad, hard chest and heard the rhythm of his heart.

"Will you promise me something?"

The rumble of his voice tickled her ear. "I'll promise you anything," she answered.

"Promise that with or without me, you'll come back here someday."

She pulled back and gazed up at him, at his strong jawline, at his dark eyes, now even darker with only stars to light his face. "Sorry . . . I can't promise you that. Without you, I won't want to come back here. This place is wonderful, but only because you're here with me."

He kissed her then, drawing her mouth to his, and suddenly it felt as if all the stars in the sky above had sprinkled themselves upon her. "Luke . . . ," she whispered.

"My love," he whispered back.

Julie and Diedra shopped for dresses on Rodeo Drive for the upcoming wedding. Julie couldn't believe the prices, or the rows of limousines parked in front of the stores. "I never knew there were so many rich people in the world," she told Diedra as they sat in a trendy restaurant having lunch.

"Out here, you get a warped perspective of wealth and material things. Don't let it dazzle you."

"I won't. But if Luke gets to play for the NFL someday, he'll be rich."

"Is that what he wants to do?"

"Yes—although his illness sort of sidetracked him. But now that he's well, I think he'll start wanting the things he used to want again."

"Does he talk about it much? About how having gotten cancer makes him feel?"

"We're both angry about it. It isn't fair, you know."

Diedra set her fork down. "Life's never fair. Sometimes we're lucky enough to find someone to love and who loves us, but 'fairly' isn't the way God runs the world."

Julie nodded. "Still, Luke gets down. I think he's afraid his cancer will come back. I tell him he's well, but still he gets depressed about it."

"You should let him talk to you," Diedra said, sipping her water. "I remember how much my mother needed to talk to me about her dying."

"But Luke's not dying."

"It doesn't matter—he still needs to get out his feelings, and because he loves you, you're the one who needs to help him talk about them."

"It's depressing for me too. I don't want him to talk about dying."

"I'd never tell you what to do, Julie, but think about it. Think about listening, really listening to his heart."

Julie pondered Diedra's advice long and hard, and two days later, when Steve and Diedra were called in for a planning session on their upcoming film project, Luke suggested he and Julie strike out on their own.

"Where are we going?" she asked as he started up Diedra's sports car. She had lent it to them for the day.

"You'll think I'm nuts, but more than anything, I want to visit Marilyn Monroe's
grave."

Julie gulped, then said cheerfully, "If that's
what you want to do, let's go."

"It's what I want to do." Luke put the car
into gear and they drove off into the hot Los
Angeles morning.

17

Julie juggled a map of Los Angeles while Luke piloted the car out onto the expressways. "Do we know where we're going?" she asked.

"I think so," he said. "I asked Steve for directions before he left."

The overhead sun blazed down and the wind blew over the open convertible, tangling Julie's hair.

"You're beautiful," Luke yelled above the roar of the engine. With his free hand, he touched her blond hair, struck golden by the rays of the sun.

"You're prejudiced," she countered.

He got off the expressway and drove down a busy thoroughfare. Eventually, he turned and stopped the car near a small, neatly kept church. He opened her door and led her through the church's parking lot, along the side of the building, through a wrought-iron gate, and into a small cemetery. The grounds were neat and well maintained, with walkways that led in orderly directions.

"Are you sure this is it?" she asked. Somehow, she had expected Marilyn Monroe to be buried in some soaring mausoleum of marble and whitewashed granite, not off some side street in the middle of a business district.

"I'm sure," Luke told her. He stopped in front of an above-ground crypt.

Carved in the stone, along with the dates of her birth and death, was Marilyn's name. The letters looked stark and surreal to Julie, and she felt goose bumps rise along her arms. She thought of all the posters she'd seen of the famous movie star, even movies she'd watched with Luke starring Marilyn, yet those images seemed far less real than her name etched in granite—perhaps because, Julie mused, behind the wall of the enclosure lay her mortal body.

Julie touched the letters gingerly. "These are different from the letters in the sidewalk," she said.

"These are final," Luke observed. "When you see somebody's signature, you expect them to be alive. But these are carved out for a person. The person doesn't have any control over these."

"Why did she get buried here? Her grave seems so ordinary for someone so popular."

"Joe DiMaggio, one of her ex-husbands, arranged this. He decided that since her life had been so public, her death and burial should be private. He loved her, even though they were divorced."

Julie honestly didn't want to be discussing death with Luke, but she recalled Diedra's urging her to listen if Luke ever wanted to discuss his feelings. And she realized that his need to see Marilyn Monroe's grave was somehow connected to his feelings about what was happening to him. "I wonder if he still loves her."

"It's hard to say. I do know that after she died, a red rose was put on her crypt every day. Every day for twenty-five years."

"Wow . . . that's awesome." Julie thought about how much she loved receiving flowers from Luke. "Too bad Marilyn couldn't let the sender know what it meant to her."

"Julie, do you think when people die they can communicate with the people they love who are still alive?"

She considered his question, then said, "I

don't think so, Luke. I think death takes people out of this world forever and that there's no way back. But I do believe in heaven, a place where souls go and where people meet again after death. Don't you believe that?"

His eyes clouded. "Sometimes I believe it. But other times, I'm afraid it's not true and that death is the end of ourselves. That we just stop existing. And we're gone forever."

She shook her head. "I'd rather not believe that way. If that's true, then why do we ever get to live? Why even *bother* to live? I like to think everybody gets to meet up again in heaven."

"I hope you're right."

She could tell he was troubled by questions he couldn't express, by mysteries he couldn't understand. She wanted to help him, but didn't know how. She didn't want to think about death and eternity, and she didn't want him thinking about it either. Regardless of what Diedra said, he was too young to talk about dying, and according to his doctors, his cancer was in remission, so she couldn't see the necessity.

She touched his arm, half to reassure herself that he was still flesh and blood. "Enough of this talk, Luke. Why don't we talk about lunch instead?"

He grinned. "Okay, so I got a little heavy. But I've been thinking more and more about things I never thought about before I got sick. I don't mean to be gloomy or to scare you."

"No problem. I guess it's only natural to think about this stuff when you've had a close call, or a serious illness, but you're fine now and so I think you should be considering next football season and how hard my father's going to be pushing you. Now *that's* scary."

"True. He's expecting me to take our team to the state finals. I hope I can."

"I know you will." She offered him a dazzling smile and took his hand. "Why don't you say good-bye to Marilyn and let's blow this place. Steve and Diedra promised to be home in time to take us to the Hard Rock Cafe for supper."

He draped his arm over her shoulders and, without so much as a backward glance, he led her away from the grave of Marilyn, away from the cemetery, and away from all the images of death that haunted him. Julie felt relief. For now, it seemed that he had closed the book on his shadowy thoughts of nonexistence and was content to walk in the light of the sun.

That weekend, Steve and Diedra took them hiking in the foothills. They left the city before daylight and were on the trail as the sun began to rise. Eastward, the indigo-blue sky faded to a paler shade of blue and streaks of pink heralded the dawn. Stars began to disappear, and slowly light reached brightening fingers across the rugged landscape and lit dark rock formations, one by one, like candles on a cake.

Julie was cold, but in an hour, as the day chased away the night, warmth spread over her like butter on warm toast. "I'm hungry," she announced finally.

"We're just about to stop and fix breakfast," Steve said, removing his backpack. "We'll need some firewood. Diedra, Luke, fan out and collect some sticks."

Wearily, Julie sat on a nearby rock. "What are we going to eat? Roadkill?"

"Bacon and eggs," Steve said, taking utensils out of his knapsack.

"You're kidding!" Julie exclaimed, pleased.

"*Powdered* eggs," Diedra said. "Sometimes not as good-tasting as roadkill."

"Do you doubt my culinary skills, woman?"

"Never." Diedra winked at Julie and Luke, who had dumped an armload of sticks and twigs at Steve's feet. "Actually, he's fed me before, and he does a passable job."

"I hope so," Luke said. "I'm hungry enough to eat the dirt off my boots."

"Which is one of our chef's most famous delicacies," Diedra joked. "And one of his best-kept secrets as to how he makes people believe he's a skilled chef. He allows his guests to get so hungry that no matter what he serves, they think it's wonderful."

"Talent such as mine doesn't need your grief," Steve announced, feigning hurt.

"Just cook," Diedra said.

In no time, Steve had the fire built, fresh coffee boiling, and bacon frying. Julie never remembered anything smelling so delicious, and she cleaned her plate greedily once breakfast was served.

"Where do we go from here?" Luke wanted to know as they put out the fire and packed up the utensils.

Steve pointed toward a flat stretch of land. Beyond it, rocks rose in jagged patterns. "In those canyons is some of the most beautiful wilderness on the face of the earth. We'll spend two hours going in, two coming out. Then back to the Jeep, and home."

The Jeep was parked at a communal parking area, miles away. "Why don't you go on and pick me up on the way back," Julie said with a yawn.

"This from a female who practically walked my legs off on Rodeo Drive," Diedra teased.

"That was different."

Luke grinned. "Yeah . . . out here there aren't any 'Sale' signs."

"Very funny." She rose to her feet. "All right, I'll show you all how tough I am." She marched off toward the canyons. Luke followed.

An hour later, she was very tired, but the stark beauty of the terrain held her interest. The four of them began to climb. The going was slow and the footing difficult, mostly because the ground was loose and Julie's boots kept sinking. Pebbles splattered behind her with every step.

"The view at the top is worth it," Steve insisted.

Winded, Julie muttered, "It had better be."

Luke, obviously in good shape again, didn't seem to mind the climb one bit. When at last

Julie hoisted herself onto level ground, she heaved a breath, then stared at the view below. Gullies and ravines wound through magnificent rock formations as far as her eye could see. In the bright sunlight, the rocks looked gardenlike, blooming in red and gold and white. Purple shadows cut swaths along the ravines and faded to black when the sunlight failed to penetrate the twists and turns.

"Wow," Julie said.

"Unbelievable," Luke said, standing next to her.

Wind, moaning in the ghostly gullies, was the only sound.

"If a person got lost in there, how'd he ever find his way out?" Luke asked.

"He might not," Diedra said. "That's why it's safest to climb up and look down on it."

"Shout something," Steve said. "Go ahead. Don't be shy."

Luke stepped forward and, cupping a hand around his mouth, yelled, "Luke loves Julie!"

The sound bounced off the canyon walls, reverberated, slid into the ravines, and finally evaporated into the air. Julie smiled at him, stepped closer to the rim, and shouted, "Julie loves Luke!"

Again, the words ricocheted back, rolling

waves of sound on a river of wind. "Julie and Luke forever!" Luke yelled. The words leaped back toward them, loud, then soft, then softer and softer before fading away.

"One more time, together?" Luke asked, taking her hand.

They lifted their arms and shouted "I love you" in unison, blending their voices and words until the two became as one. And they listened as their words returned to them, until the echoes of their words became as embedded in the memory of the canyon as the colors of the sun.

18

When Luke and Julie were four days away from leaving Los Angeles, Steve and Diedra made the final preparations for their wedding. The day before the ceremony, the four of them drove north along the coastal highway, toward Monterey and the centuries-old chapel that Steve had reserved for the wedding.

The road hugged the shoreline and, from the backseat of the Mercedes, Julie watched the ocean sweep across coarse-grained beaches of sand and, where there was no beach, watched the salty water smash into soaring, craggy cliffs of rugged granite. Steve turned east, into the hills, and drove over a ridge into a sunny, sleepy valley, seemingly untouched by time, that cradled a quiet town.

The chapel, in the center of the town, was a

rectangular adobe building with a bell tower and an ancient mission bell that monks rang every morning and at twilight. There was a single main street, lined with boutiques, gourmet food shops, and colorful craft stores selling Native American and Mexican artwork.

Steve had arranged for two rooms at a quaint bed-and-breakfast inn—Julie and Diedra in one room, he and Luke in another. They ate supper on the back patio, under trellises draped with night-blooming jasmine and moonflowers. A man playing a Spanish guitar strolled among the tables, serenading the diners.

They ate leisurely, lingering over coffee and dessert, enjoying the balmy night breeze that gently stirred the petals of the flowers and sent sweet, subtle scents across the patio. Julie kept gazing up at the stars, which were spread out across the sky like jewels on black velvet. She could hardly believe that in two days, she and Luke would fly back home and California would be only a memory. She heard Luke ask, "You two going to go on a honeymoon?"

"We head for Europe at the end of next month for our next film project," Steve replied. "We thought we'd grab our honeymoon before we have to start work."

"Where?" Julie asked, thinking how romantic it sounded to honeymoon in Europe.

"London, first," Diedra said. "Then Paris and Madrid. We'll be filming in Spain, so that's where we'll end up."

"How long will you be gone?" Luke asked.

"Almost four months," Steve said. "We've got to hunt out locations before we start filming. And once we wrap up the European project, we head on to Japan for the next one. We probably won't be back in the States until next spring."

Julie sighed. "High school sounds so boring by comparison."

"It's a long time to be away from home," Diedra said. "Especially when all we really want to do is settle down and have kids."

Steve took her hand. "And that's just what we're going to do once the Japanese project is over."

Diedra smiled at him and, sensing their tender bond, Julie reached for Luke's hand. She was surprised to see Luke studying his uncle with an expression of sadness. She wondered what he was thinking and feeling, but she didn't get the opportunity to ask because as soon as dinner was finished, she and Diedra returned to their room amid talk of tomorrow being the "big day."

While Diedra took a shower, Julie lay on her bed staring moodily into space, wondering about Luke. The phone rang and she grabbed the receiver. Luke's voice said, "Julie, meet me in the chapel tomorrow morning at ten."

"The wedding's not until one."

"I know, but I want to talk to you before the wedding. And I don't want to be rushed."

The inn wasn't far from the chapel. According to local legend, in olden days a bride would walk barefoot from the center of town to the church, where her groom would be waiting. "Is something wrong?" Julie asked, feeling a flutter of fear.

"I just want to talk to you," Luke said. "Please. It's important."

Wild horses couldn't have kept her away. And so the next morning, promising a nervous Diedra she'd be back in time for lunch, Julie hurried down the quiet street to the chapel. She pushed open the timeworn wooden door. Inside, the air was cool, candles glowed on the altar, and small rectangular windows allowed sunlight to filter into the darkness. She waited for her eyes to adjust and saw Luke sitting in a pew near the front.

She slid in beside him. "Hi," she whispered, for although they were alone, she hesitated to break the reverent quiet. "What's up?"

He turned to her and took her in his arms. "I wanted to be alone with you here, before the wedding and all."

She returned his hug and felt her anxiety evaporate. "Well, here I am."

Luke shifted in the pew, and Julie could tell that something was troubling him. All at once, he asked, "What if you could never have babies, Julie? Would that make you not want to marry someone?"

Caught totally off guard by his question, Julie fumbled for an answer. "Gee, Luke, I haven't even decided what college I want to attend. It's hard to think about having babies and what I might want years and years from now."

"But it's important. I—I need to know."

"Did all of Steve's talk about kids make you think too much about your future? You know, like the day we went to Marilyn Monroe's grave?"

He shook his head. "It started me thinking about what my doctor told us about the radiation possibly making me sterile. It made me wonder if getting married knowing I might not be able to give a woman kids would make her not want to marry me in the first place."

"If having kids is the most important thing, then maybe it would make a difference. But no one knows if they're able to have kids until they start trying. I guess if babies are *that* important to a couple, and they can't have their own, then they adopt. It seems like the world's full of unwanted babies."

"That's true, but I want to know how important having children is to *you.*"

"Why?"

"Because I love you, Julie."

"I love you too."

"Because I want to marry you."

The atmosphere in the chapel became charged, and Julie could scarcely hold in her breath. Her heart hammered against her rib cage. "Didn't you ask me that in sixth grade?"

He smiled at the memory, easing the tension. "Yes, and you said, 'Get lost, bozo.'"

"Ouch! Was I that mean?"

"You've made up for it."

"So is this a bona fide marriage proposal?"

He took her hand. "There's never been anybody else for me except you, Julie Ellis. And there never will be."

Her heart melted. "And you're afraid I

might not want to marry you if I know you might not be able to have children?"

"You should have a choice."

"*You're* my choice," she said softly.

A smile of joy and relief lit his face. "That's what I wanted you to say. You already told me that the cancer didn't matter to you, but I had to know for sure how you felt about this baby thing."

"Now you know."

He straightened his leg, dug in the pocket of his jeans, and withdrew a small box. "This is for you."

Heart pounding, she opened it and saw a ring of fine silver, intricately carved, with a turquoise set in its center. "It's gorgeous," she whispered.

"It's Mexican. According to folklore, long ago, before soldiers went off to war, they gave this kind of ring to their special girl as a signal to others she was taken."

"So is this my engagement ring?"

"It's a promise ring." Luke removed it from the box and slipped it onto the third finger of her left hand. "It's a promise that someday I'll buy you a diamond engagement ring, when I can really plan on marrying you. I know you have college ahead and I know your mother will kill me if you don't go."

Tears filmed her eyes as she held out her hand to stare at the ring. "We both have college," she reminded him.

"Well, the jury's still out about my future."

"Don't say that!" Her tone was urgent. "You can't promise to marry me and then say you might not have a future. I won't hear it."

"Knowing that you want to marry me someday gives me more to look forward to than anything else ever could," he said in an attempt to calm her.

"Even more than playing football?"

"Football's only a game. *You* are real life." He leaned forward and, in the quiet sanctity of the chapel, he kissed her lovingly on her lips.

Hours later, Julie returned to the chapel with a nervous Diedra and Steve. Since the ceremony was to be small and unattended, Diedra didn't walk down the aisle. She joined Steve at the altar in front of the priest while a guitarist played haunting Spanish music.

Julie thought Diedra looked beautiful in a simple white summer dress of eyelet lace. A white-lace Spanish mantilla covered her head and flowed down her shoulders. Her bouquet was made up of lilies mixed with pale purple orchids. Steve's eyes shone as he gazed at her, reminding Julie of candles alight with fire.

Julie wore a sundress in the palest shade of butter yellow, carried a bouquet of daisies and gardenias, and quivered with excitement and anticipation. Someday, *she* would be the bride, and Luke her groom.

Luke stood beside Steve, looking lean and fit in a navy-blue suit. The family resemblance between nephew and uncle was striking. During the speaking of the vows, Luke caught Julie's eye, and it was as if every word the priest spoke was meant for them also: *". . . for richer, for poorer, in sickness and in health, 'til death do us part."*

The words took on new meaning for Julie. Getting married was a serious business—a life-and-death commitment. A pledge to be joined with one other person for all of earthly time. And when the person you loved, as she loved Luke, already had a life-threatening illness, the promise seemed even more profound.

She locked gazes with Luke and saw his love for her shining in his eyes. She smiled, hoping to communicate that she was willing to make such a commitment to him. That she was willing to stand by him no matter what his future held.

She fingered the silver and turquoise ring on her finger—his promise ring. Silently, she promised to love and stick by him until they could say their vows before God and formally pledge their love for all time.

19

Julie and Luke returned home to a crowd of family and friends waiting for them at the airport. Everyone was glad to see them and everyone started questioning them at once about their trip. Julie's father reminded Luke about upcoming preseason practice, Luke's mother eagerly sorted through photos of Steve and Diedra, and kids from school wanted to know who they'd seen who was famous.

The hawk eye of Julie's mother fell on the ring, which Julie brushed off as a souvenir, but when Solena came over to her house the next morning, Julie told her the truth.

"A promise ring! Oh, Julie, that's so-o-o romantic."

"When he gave it to me in that chapel, my heart almost stopped." Julie held out her hand, allowing the ring to catch the light of the morning sun coming through her bedroom window. "I'm never going to take it off."

"This means you're practically engaged. Are you sure you can wait to get married until you're out of college? That's years from now."

"I know, but Luke should have a chance to play college ball and I really would like to have some kind of career. If you could have met Diedra and seen how cool she was, you'd understand. Besides, now that Luke and I are sure that we want to get married, we can take our time about it. But you're right—it *is* going to be hard to wait," she added wistfully.

"Well, I don't think it's fair for one person to have so much going for her. But"—Solena smiled—"if it has to be somebody, I'm glad it's you."

"Thanks. What's hard for me now isn't thinking about college, but thinking about high school. I'm bored already, and my senior year hasn't even started." She hugged her knees to her chest and rested her chin on them. "So how was your summer? And how'd the job go? What was Jason like?"

Solena wrinkled her nose. "Waterton is mega-boring—the armpit of the Midwest.

And as for the job and Jason, well, the best I can say about the whole experience is that I got a regular paycheck."

"Pretty dull, huh?"

"Jason discovered Melanie Hawkins and spent the whole month of July trailing after her. It was disgusting! Don't guys have any self-respect?"

Julie giggled. "Well, at least that kept her away from Frank, didn't it?"

"Yes, but . . ." She jutted her lip in a pout. "It sure didn't give me a chance to have an adventure like you. And Jason is going home soon, but Melanie will still be here. So, I guess it'll be another year of keeping her away from Frank."

"You can do it, girl."

Solena made an outrageous face. "Okay, tell me more about California."

"It was the most wonderful place in the world. I never had so much fun, and because I was with Luke . . . well, that was the most special part of all."

"How's he feeling?"

"Fine. He worked out at his uncle's gym to stay in shape."

"Seeing how good he looked at the airport, it's hard to remember how bad he looked dur-

ing chemo. I'm sure this whole mess is behind
him."

"Me too," Julie said. She gazed down lovingly at the ring. "Especially now, when we
have so much going for us."

On Friday, Luke and Julie had Solena and
Frank over to her house for an all-night video
movie marathon. "Your last all-nighter," her
father told the boys. "Once practice starts, it's
back to hard work and regular hours."

In a way, Julie resented the imposition of
the schedule, but with Luke looking forward
so to resuming play, she kept her feelings to
herself. Practices were called for three hours
each morning and two hours each afternoon at
the nearby middle school field, which would
be their temporary home field for the fall season. In the grueling August heat, Luke was so
exhausted he fell asleep early each night, leaving Julie to spend her time hanging out with
her friends and getting ready for the start of
the school year.

On Labor Day, her father had his annual
barbecue bash for all the players on his team.
He fired up a massive grill in the backyard and
fed over thirty guys, from incoming freshmen
to seniors. Luke was clearly the hero of the

day. A newspaper reporter showed up, interviewed him, took pictures of Luke and the team, and told Luke there'd be a front-page story in Sunday's sports section.

Late in the afternoon, Luke whisked Julie away to the high school and the football stadium, which was still under construction. They climbed up a new set of concrete bleachers and settled on the highest tier. Below, the field appeared green, with wispy strands of grass, but the underground sprinkling system had yet to be installed and the final sod hadn't been put down. Since the growing season was all but over, it would be spring before the new turf could be installed.

"Too bad I won't get to play here," Luke said.

"This time next year, you'll be throwing for some college. Daddy says the Tulane coach has contacted him about you."

"Tulane and Ohio State. I wish I could play for both of them."

"I've never seen Dad so eager about the start of a new season. He's driving me and Mom crazy with football talk."

Luke puckered his brow. "Everybody's counting on me, Julie. I hope I don't let them down."

"You'll do just fine. Just make sure you don't get hurt."

He grinned. "Frank's my main man up front, and he says he'll take off anybody's head who sacks me."

"And if he doesn't, he'll have Solena and me to face."

"That'll keep him scared enough to do his job."

"It better." She twined her fingers through his. "I got a postcard from Steve and Diedra in Paris."

"Me too. They sound like they're having a ball."

"Diedra says that she wishes we were with them and that when we take a honeymoon, we have to include Paris on the tour. What do you think?"

"I think we'll be lucky to afford Parris Island, South Carolina."

"Are you kidding? By then, you'll be a Heisman Trophy winner and a first-round draft pick for the NFL."

"I like the way you think, Julie," he said with a laugh. "I've dreamed about playing pro ball since I was a kid."

"You still should."

He shrugged. "Let's face it, I may not be

anyone's first choice anymore. Cancer has a way of scaring pro scouts off."

She linked her arm through his. "You're *my* first choice."

He leaned over and kissed the tip of her nose. "Then get a good education, in case you end up supporting me."

She grimaced. "Isn't it enough I get this from my mother? Do I have to get it from you too?"

"She on your case again about picking a college?"

"She's never gotten *off* my case. So give me your top three choices and I'll tell her and she can start sending off for applications."

"You're really serious about going wherever I go?"

"Of course. Unless you want to be separated for four years."

"Not hardly." He studied her face. "It's just that I want you to do what you really want— not feel tied down by promises you made to me."

She held out her hand. "Then this ring doesn't mean anything?"

"It means I love you and want to marry you."

"That's what *I* want. And so going to a college far away from you isn't likely."

The sky was darkening, threatening rain. "We'd better head for home before we get drenched," he said, pulling her to her feet.

They hurried down the steps and onto the field. The ground was lumpy and hard. Julie jogged ahead to the center of the field, stopped, and tried to imagine what it would be like to play a game with hundreds of people cheering and yelling her name. She couldn't. Yet for Luke, she knew, it was a common occurrence.

Luke came alongside, picked up a stick, tossed it high in the air, and caught it while she cheered. "Our first game is against Hammond next Friday. Your father thinks we'll wipe up the field with them."

"One thing my father knows is football," Julie said. "If he thinks we'll win, we probably will."

Luke gazed over the field, letting his vision sweep from one end to the other. "Yep, this is going to be one fine field." He took the stick and scrawled symbols in the dirt. He made the letter I, drew a heart, and then scrawled the letter U. It was the same "I love you" message he'd carved on Julie's backyard tree the previous May.

"Don't let my dad see you marking up his field," she teased. "He'll have a fit. Football players are supposed to be tough, not sissies who fall in love."

His eyes twinkled. "Is that what I am, a sissy?"

"A wimp," she said, as large drops of rain began to splat against the ground.

"You call me—a guy who's going to be on the front page of the sports section—a wimp?"

Playfully, she stuck out her tongue and darted off.

He chased her down and began tickling her sides. "Who's a wimp?"

Julie shrieked with laughter and fell to the ground, rolling every which way to evade his fingers. Rain fell in sheets, stinging Julie's skin and soaking them both. In minutes they were streaked with mud, but Julie didn't care.

Pressing her to the ground with his body, Luke pinned her arms over her head. "Beg for mercy," he said above the sound of the pouring rain.

"Never," she cried.

Water streamed off him and his eyes looked like glowing coals. Julie felt a surge of fire course through her body and was surprised that her skin wasn't sizzling with the heat. "Then suffer the consequences," he said.

He lowered his mouth to hers and kissed her long and deep while the rain washed over them and thunder clapped in the sky.

20

By the end of September, the Waterton Warriors were 5 and 0 and ranked number one in their division in the state. Luke got most of the credit for team leadership, while being lauded for keeping a cool head under pressure and for his golden throwing arm, and Julie had never seen her father more excited about a team. "This is it, Julie," he'd say each morning after a victory. "I've waited for this team for over twenty years. They're the best. And Luke is absolutely the finest player I've ever coached—one in a million."

"I agree, Dad," she'd reply. "He's one in a million." But for Julie, his stellar status had little to do with football. She loved him so much it was becoming increasingly difficult to think about waiting until they both finished college to get married.

Meanwhile, her mother never let up on her about college. To appease her, Julie sent off for applications to Tulane and Ohio State. "Why Tulane?" her mother asked.

"Why not? You said I should get away from this area."

"Well, what course of study are you interested in taking? Some colleges concentrate more on one area than another. If I know what you're interested in, I can do a computer search for the schools that offer your area of interest and you can apply to them."

"I'm not sure. Isn't it enough I'm picking some colleges without having to determine the entire course of my college career before I even begin?"

"That's not what I mean."

"Can we just drop it, Mom?"

Her mother studied her thoughtfully, and said, "I'm not stupid, Julie. I know you're ambivalent because you want to wait and see where Luke chooses to attend."

Julie saw no reason to argue about it. "So what? Only the best colleges are recruiting him, so it's not as if I'll pick a bad one."

"You need to choose a college based on your needs—not Luke's."

"Mother, please, stop it. I'm doing the best that I can."

Frustrated, her mother turned her back and swept from the room.

Julie was at the mall one Saturday afternoon when she ran into Luke's mother. They went to the food court, ordered frozen yogurt, and sat together to eat it. "I don't get to see much of you anymore," Nancy said between bites. "If it weren't for home games, I doubt I'd see you at all."

"I miss coming over. Blame my dad. He's so fixated on this season, he practically keeps the team under lock and key. It's so-o-o frustrating."

Nancy smiled. "You think you're frustrated. You should see Luke pacing the floor wishing he could be with you."

The news thrilled Julie. She liked knowing Luke missed being with her. "He has a lot of pressure on him."

"That's true, and I've mentioned to him that he shouldn't be too intense, that the entire fate of the football season doesn't rest on his shoulders. It looks to me as if he's losing weight, and I'm afraid he's worrying too much about the season."

Julie set down her spoon. "But he's feeling all right, isn't he?"

"He says he is."

Seeing Nancy's concern upset Julie. "He told me his checkup went fine. It did, didn't it?"

"I haven't heard otherwise."

Ironically, on the day Luke had been scheduled to go into Chicago for testing, Nancy had had an office review by the corporate bigwigs and Julie had been scheduled to take her SAT exams. Luke insisted that he could go through the routine without them and that if there were any problems with his blood work or bone scans, he'd be notified. The day after, the Warriors had played one of their top rivals and Luke had led them to another victory.

Julie picked up her spoon and dug into her frozen dessert. "Well, I'm sure that if anything were wrong, you'd have been notified by Dr. Kessler."

"You're right. Luke says I shouldn't obsess about every little lost pound or sniffle he has." Nancy smiled wanly. "I know he's right, but it's hard for me not to. Last winter and spring were the longest days of my life. I just couldn't believe Luke was having such problems. He's always been perfectly healthy."

"We shouldn't think about those bad times. The important thing is that he's fine now and on the way to the rest of his life." Julie smiled. "And I'm glad to be going along for the ride."

Nancy laughed. "I don't know what he'd do without you, Julie. He's been crazy about you since he was just a little kid."

"That's nice of you to say. I'm crazy about him, too."

The food court tables had filled with the lunch crowd while they'd been talking, and the smells of fast food hung in the air. Nancy glanced nervously from side to side. "Um—I don't mean to pry, but I am curious about some things."

"Ask me."

"You and Luke have discussed marriage, haven't you?"

Now it was Julie's turn to cast a nervous glance. "I suppose we have."

"Don't be concerned: I'm not against it. But I really do want Luke to go to college."

"He'll go," Julie assured her. "How could he not go with all these college football coaches after him?"

Nancy smiled and relaxed. "How indeed!

I'm glad, Julie. I want so many things for Luke, and he's so close to getting some of them."

Julie understood, and only wished her own mother could be as flexible as Luke's. "I won't take his dreams away," she said.

"Please don't think I'm prying or trying to tell you what to do. One of the things he wants—that he's always wanted—is you. And I won't interfere with any plans the two of you've made."

"It's all right," Julie insisted. "Luke and I plan to have it *all.*"

Nancy's round face broke into a broad smile. "And you will. I'm positive of that. With all that the two of you have going for you, you'll have everything life has to offer."

Julie basked in Nancy's approval, only wishing that Luke were there to share it. That night, the Warriors would play their homecoming game, and afterward, there was to be a dance in the gym. Luke would be taking her and there'd be no early curfew, so she could spend hours with him. Snapping out of her reverie, Julie said, "Sit with Solena, Mom, and me at the game tonight."

"I'd love to," Luke's mother responded.

"After all, this one's against the Trojans,

and I think we should all be together when Luke hands them their first loss of the season."

That night, the air was crisp and cold, perfect for playing football. The middle school stands were packed to overflowing, as the Warriors-Trojans game was one of northwest Indiana's great rivalries. TV cameras and newspaper photographers had special field passes and crews were set up along one end zone.

In the stands, behind the Warriors' bench on the fifty-yard line, Julie watched Luke warm up on the field throwing passes as her father paced furiously along the sidelines.

"So where do you think they are?" Solena asked, craning her neck at the crowds sitting behind them.

"Who?"

"The college scouts! Frank said the stands would be crawling with them for tonight's game."

Julie's father had told her the same thing. But Julie wasn't interested in talking about scouts. She kept her gaze on Luke, who seemed to be having trouble with his passes.

Following her line of vision, Solena said, "I'm sure he's just nervous. Wait 'til the game starts."

Yet, when the game started, Luke didn't improve. Only a clever play by the defense kept the Trojans from going out in front during the second quarter. Julie anxiously twisted the blanket across her lap. Luke couldn't blow it now. Not with so many important people watching.

She saw her father call Luke to the sidelines and lecture him sternly. Luke had ripped off his helmet and Julie could see that he was grimacing and sweating profusely. "I wish Daddy would get off Luke's case," she said to her mother irritably.

"Never tell your father how to coach a game," her mother said. "One way or another he gets the best from his boys. And Luke's his pride and joy."

Her mother's words didn't comfort Julie, whose mood only darkened when Luke took a hard hit minutes before the half ended. "Where was his protection?" she shouted, springing to her feet. She glared down at Solena. "Frank's supposed to cover him!"

"Don't yell at *me*," Solena exclaimed.

Angry and agitated, Julie sat down, only to watch Luke being helped off the field and taken to the locker room. The announcer commented about Luke being shaken up on the play, and Julie's anger turned to anxiety. She longed to rush off to the gym, but knew she'd never get inside. "He'll be all right," she heard Nancy say.

Mercifully, the half ended and Coach Ellis jogged with his team off the field. The roar of the crowd dropped to a lull. "Popcorn?" Patricia Ellis asked.

Julie shook her head and snapped, "How can you ask about popcorn when Luke's hurt?"

"I'll go with you," Nancy said, heading off an argument.

Julie's mother and Nancy stood, but didn't leave, because someone called their names. Julie turned to see Brett Carney, one of the new freshmen on the team, hurrying toward them. He was in his uniform, but because he hadn't played, his jersey was clean and unmarked. "Coach sent me," Brett said, climbing up the few rows to where they sat.

"What's wrong with Luke?" Julie asked as her heart thudded rapidly in her chest. "I know something's wrong. Tell me."

Brett's eyes were wide as saucers and his skin looked pale, as if he'd had a great fright. "Luke collapsed in the locker room," Brett said. "He's being taken to the hospital."

"Which one?" Nancy asked.

"Waterton General."

Julie grabbed for her purse and car keys, but her mother pulled them from her hands, then took both Julie and Nancy firmly by their elbows and said, "Come on. I'll drive."

21

"Why is it taking so long?" Julie paced the floor of the emergency room waiting area like a caged cat.

"I'm sure the doctors have to check him over completely," her mother said in an attempt to calm her down.

Even Luke's mother hadn't been allowed behind the doors to the room where Luke was being examined. She sat tight-lipped on the edge of a chair, clutching her hands nervously in her lap.

"Don't they know we're worried? Don't they know how hard it is to wait and wait?" Julie continued to pace. Her hands felt clammy and cold and her heart raced. "I wish Daddy were here."

"You know he'll be here as soon as he can get away from the game."

"That stupid game is the cause of all this," Julie cried.

Solena, who'd insisted on coming to offer Julie whatever support she could, said nothing and watched Julie pace.

A doctor emerged from behind the treatment room doors. "Are you with Luke Muldenhower?"

"I want to see my son." Nancy hurried to the doctor's side. "What's wrong with him? How is he?"

"He has a concussion," the doctor said. "He's alert, but extremely fatigued, and we want to hold him overnight for observation and keep a check on his vital signs. He's being moved upstairs to a room. Dr. Portage has been notified and will be here soon to check on your son."

Julie remembered the doctor who'd first treated Luke for the infection that had become Hodgkin's. At least he was familiar with Luke, and she was glad that Luke would be with a doctor he knew. "Where's his room?" she asked.

When they were allowed to see Luke, it was all Julie could do to hold back until after his mother had fussed over him. When it was Julie's turn, she put her arms around him and buried her face in his neck. "Oh, Luke, I've been so scared."

"I got hit, and then I got dizzy and fell in the locker room. I don't remember much, except that I was playing lousy."

Julie thought he looked pale, and in spite of the coolness of the room, he was perspiring. "Just so long as you're all right."

"We're going to lose the game because of me."

"Forget the game. It doesn't matter now."

"It matters to me."

They stayed with him until her father arrived. He barreled into the room and tore to Luke's bedside. Julie saw worry lines etched in his brow. "Got here as soon as I could. How're you doing, son?"

"Did we lose?" was all Luke wanted to know.

"Hey, you win some, you lose some. That's the way the game goes."

"So we lost." Luke turned his head toward the wall.

"Don't worry about it. We'll meet them again in the district playoffs and we'll kick butt."

Luke didn't seem mollified. "And how about the scouts? I guess they saw me play the worst game of my career."

"One game won't make or break your future, Luke. They'll be back."

"They'll say I blew it when it mattered, when I was under pressure."

"No they won't. Stop stewing about it. Get some rest, and as soon as the doctors say you can go back to playing, you will. You might miss one game at the most."

"I'll miss more than that," Luke said enigmatically. His dark eyes looked so unbearably sad that Julie felt cold fingers of fear squeeze her heart.

"Not because of a little bump on the head," Bud Ellis said. "Wait and see."

"Sure," Luke answered. "Whatever you say, Coach."

"Something's come up in Luke's blood work," Dr. Portage told Luke's mother the following day when she and Julie had come to visit Luke. He'd caught them just as they were about to go into Luke's room.

"What do you mean?"

"I'm having his radiologist look over some

X rays and test results, and I've ordered a bone marrow aspiration."

Julie felt sick to her stomach, as if someone had punched her. She heard Nancy say, "But he just had that battery of tests at St. Paul's in Chicago last month."

"No he didn't." Dr. Portage closed the chart he'd been holding and looked at Luke's mother gravely. "I called and asked for some of his records to be sent over. His last checkup at St. Paul's was in June."

Julie reeled at the news. That was before she and Luke had gone to Los Angeles. "But he said he'd been checked," she blurted. "He told me he'd gone by train and gotten his checkup."

"Well, he didn't," Dr. Portage said. "According to their records, he never went."

"Why did you lie to me, Luke?"

Julie watched Luke's face as his mother asked her question. He looked ashamed and pale. Ghostly pale. "I rescheduled my appointment, that's all. I was feeling good and so I figured I could postpone it for a while. I would have gone as soon as football season was over."

"Football season! Since when is football more important than your health?"

He looked helplessly at Julie, who struggled to hold back tears. "Everybody was expecting so much from me. I—I didn't want to let them down."

"Who would you have let down? Everybody knew you'd been sick. Nobody held you accountable."

"Mom, please, I'm not up to fighting about this. I feel awful right now."

Nancy's expression didn't soften, but before she could speak, Dr. Portage called her out of the room and Julie found herself alone with Luke. She crossed her arms and dabbed at her eyes. "I would have skipped my SATs and gone with you, if you'd asked," she told him. "Why didn't you ask me?"

"I told you, I would have gone later."

"Did my dad put pressure on you? Because if he did—"

"Julie, stop it. Everybody put pressure on me! Don't you understand?"

"*I* didn't pressure you. I only want you to play football because it means so much to *you.*"

Luke pulled himself up and hoisted his legs over the side of the bed, grunting in discomfort. He took a few deep breaths and stared at Julie, his dark eyes made darker by the paleness of his skin. He looked miserable. "It's true you never pressured me to play ball, but you put plenty of pressure on me to be well."

"How? When? I never did."

"You tell me all the time, 'Now that you're over cancer,' and, 'You're fine . . . time to get on with your life.' "

Stricken by his words, stunned by his accusation, Julie began to recall all the times she'd said such things. "But I was only trying to be positive. I was only trying to encourage you."

"Don't you think I want to be well, Julie? Don't you think I want to be rid of this and be normal? And play ball? And marry you? Don't you think if being positive would make me well, I would be well?"

Tears spilled down her cheeks as his words fell like blows. "But the tests—"

"I had one good checkup after my radiation treatments. Then I had the best summer of my life, with you, and then I had to face going back for more testing and maybe hearing that I was sick again. And everybody wanted me to be well so much. And *I* wanted it so much." He hung his head and took deep breaths before continuing. "So it was easy to put off going for the testing. Maybe I figured what I didn't know wouldn't hurt me."

She ached for him, for herself. "Oh, Luke . . ."

"I told myself there'd be time to get check-ups after the season was over. After the team went to the state finals. I wanted that so bad, Julie. So, I kept playing, kept ignoring what was happening, even when the symptoms started coming back."

"You've been sick?"

He shrugged, refused to meet her gaze. "First it was the fatigue. Then the night sweats. I washed my sheets so Mom wouldn't know. I knew I was in trouble, but I kept pushing myself. I didn't want to let anybody down. I didn't want to find out the truth."

"That you're out of remission," she finished flatly. She felt as if someone had pulled a plug on her emotions and drained them all away.

"Yes."

"Do you know it for sure?"

He looked up and held her blue eyes with the dark pull of his own. "I know how I feel, Julie; I've been here before. And in ER, once they read my chart and saw that I'd been treated for Hodgkin's, they wanted to do a bone marrow. That's not a routine test for a head injury, you know."

She looked at her hands, at the promise ring that now seemed to mock her, to ridicule all it had stood for between her and Luke. "I'm sorry if I caused you any harm by insisting that you be well. I didn't mean to make you skip your testing."

For the first time since they'd been talking, Luke reached out and touched Julie. He smoothed her hair and ran his fingers tenderly along her cheek. "I'm not blaming you. I would never blame you. It was my choice. Coach always taught us to take responsibility." He offered a humorless chuckle. "No, I knew the chance I was taking; I knew the consequences. All testing would have done was confirm what I already knew."

Fresh tears spilled from Julie's eyes, and slowly Luke took her in his arms, where she sobbed, soaking his hospital shirt. "I love you so much," she managed between sobs.

"Loving you was all I had to hang on to sometimes. When I'd wake up at night, sweaty and nauseous, I'd remember L.A. and that church, and all the fun. It got me through."

Julie didn't know how long she had been clinging to him, but when Nancy and Dr. Portage returned to the room, she was still in Luke's arms. She pulled away reluctantly.

"Luke, we need to talk," Dr. Portage said.

The expression on Nancy's face told Julie what he was going to say before he spoke.

"There are cancer cells in your bone marrow," he said.

Luke's emotion could be seen only in a tightening along his jawline. "So where do I go from here?"

"Back to St. Paul's. They'll start looking for a compatible donor via computer in the national marrow registry. Unfortunately, the task is complicated because you have a rare blood type."

Luke didn't flinch. "Is that it?"

"They'll put you back onto chemo maintenance to inhibit the spread as much as possible until a donor's found."

"So, I guess this means that I'll be out for the rest of the season."

Luke's attempt at humor brought a thin smile to the doctor's lips. "Shall I write a note to your coach excusing you from play?"

"How about if you write one to God instead? Tell him to find me a donor." Luke pulled Julie closer to him. "Tell him I don't want to die."

22

Luke went back to St. Paul's long enough to have his chemo device implanted and his dose regulated. Upon returning home, he doggedly started school again, and his baseball hat once more became a familiar sight in the halls and classrooms.

News of his need for a bone marrow donor made the front page in the local paper and was picked up by the Associated Press national news service. He got calls, offers of money, requests for TV interviews—everything except a compatible donor. He asked for nothing, preferring to stay out of the limelight. By fielding calls and running interference, Coach Ellis saw to it that Luke and his mother weren't hounded.

At school, Frank rallied the football team, as well as the student body, and he and Solena initiated a bone marrow testing day. A doctor and three nurses came from St. Paul's with syringes and vials for blood samples, along with permission slips. Most of the students lined up after school to have their blood tested for a possible match.

Coach Ellis was first in line. Julie was second. It touched her, seeing the support and caring Luke inspired in their classmates. The paper covered that event also, but she couldn't bring herself to read the stories. They left her sad and depressed. And scared. For she knew that a bone marrow transplant was Luke's only hope for survival; he was getting sicker and balder and more gaunt from the chemo and the relentless advance of his cancer, and time, Julie knew, was running out for him. A donor had to be found—and found soon.

As October faded into November, Luke was able to attend school less and less. On the days he did come, Frank picked him up and Julie drove him home. Yet he rarely wanted to go home until they visited the new stadium, which was now almost fully constructed. Even on cold, blustery days, he insisted on going. Julie would take his hand and they'd slowly climb the new bleachers, sit, and gaze down at the field.

"I sure wish I could play football again," Luke said wistfully one November afternoon.

"If those doctors find a donor in time, you will," Julie answered.

"Don't you ever give up?"

"No. And neither should you."

He entwined his fingers with hers. "When you're up against a superior enemy, sometimes it's okay to bow out gracefully," he said quietly.

She whirled to face him. "I hate it when you talk so negatively. A donor *will* be found. And you *will* go to college and play football."

"Come on," he chided. "I don't like arguing with you." He managed one of his endearing grins. "I'm a lover, not a fighter. Remember?"

She returned her gaze to the barren, muddy field, where large clumps of dirt were riddled with bulldozer tracks. It looked brown and ugly, making it hard for her to imagine the field flat and thick with a carpet of grass. "Yes you are too a fighter. I've seen you fight to win in many a football game. And to me, your life is much more worth fighting for than any game."

"I *am* fighting for my life, Julie. I fight for it every day."

"But you talk about losing the fight, and that really scares me."

"I can't win every game I play."

"It's being on the chemo, Luke. It's getting you discouraged. Once you're off it, you'll feel better about everything."

"I promise: I won't give up." He toyed with a strand of her long hair.

Thoroughly depressed, Julie changed the subject. "Our last home game's in two weeks. Will you come? Dad wants you to."

"I'm coming," he said. "I started the season with the team, and I want to finish with them."

Without Luke, the Warriors had lost their heart to win and had quickly slipped from their number one ranking as what had been their most brilliant season turned to dust.

On the night of the game, Julie and her family picked up Luke and his mother in a specially equipped van. Too weak to walk, Luke had been given a wheelchair. "Are you sure you're up to coming?" Coach asked.

Luke settled his baseball cap and told him, "Yes. I want to go." Luke's clothes hung on him. His once-powerful physique had melted away and his body had turned skeletal as the war against cancer raged within him. Julie reminded herself that he'd regained his form after his first bout with chemo was complete and that she should have every hope it would happen again.

They drove in silence to the game and, once there, Coach Ellis positioned Luke on the field, along the sidelines, at the end of the Warriors' bench. When the team filed onto the field, each player stepped in front of Luke's wheelchair, removed his helmet, and shook Luke's hand. Julie watched from the stands, a lump in her throat, as Luke gave every player a high five, a smile, a few words.

And at halftime, she watched her father push Luke's wheelchair out to the middle of the field while the announcer recited his football exploits and the bright field lights glinted off the polished metal of his chair. Cameras flashed as the mayor and superintendent of schools stood with him. The mayor made a brief speech about how much honor Luke had brought to Waterton with his talent. He gave Luke a plaque and then announced, "In your honor, the new high school stadium will be called 'Luke Muldenhower Stadium,' and will be formally dedicated as such come spring."

Julie heard Luke's mother gasp when the announcement was made and felt Nancy reach for her hand. Tears were all but blinding Julie, but she held her head high, feeling more pride for Luke than ever. His talent might have brought him fame, but his courage in the face of cancer had brought him honor.

Spring. Julie wondered if Luke would still be waiting for a donor or if his bone marrow transplant would be history by then. *Spring.* The season of flowers and fresh green grass seemed so far away. They still had the long, harsh Indiana winter to endure. She bowed her head and whispered fervently, "Hurry up, spring."

"Julie, we need to talk." Patricia Ellis came into Julie's room, closing the door behind her.

Julie didn't mind the interruption. She'd tried valiantly all evening to study for her upcoming finals, but had been unable to concentrate. She turned down the Christmas music playing from the radio on her desk. "What's up?"

"What are you doing about your acceptances to Tulane and Ohio State?"

"What do you mean? I'm not doing anything about them."

Her mother looked confused. "You've got

to choose one of them. After all, you're graduating in six months and—"

"Mother!" Julie stood. "What are you thinking? I can't go off and leave Luke. What if he gets his donor marrow? I need to be here for him."

"Julie, are you serious? Are you telling me you're not going off to college just because Luke isn't?"

"Of course I'm serious. I wouldn't dream of leaving Luke."

A worried frown creased her mother's brow. "You can't put the rest of your life on hold for Luke's sake. I'm sure if you ask him, he'd want you to go ahead with your plans."

"My plans are to stay with Luke until he's well. If that means postponing college for a year, then that's what I'll do."

Her mother didn't back down, but her expression grew pensive. Haltingly, she said, "Luke's gravely ill, Julie. What if . . . what if a donor can't be found?"

"I think one will be found."

"But honey, what if—"

"Stop it!" Julie stamped her foot. "I won't hear all this horrible talk. Luke's *got* to get well again. I can't even think about going through the rest of my life without him. I wouldn't even *want* to!" She held out her hand. "Remember this ring? It's more than just a souvenir from my summer vacation. It's a 'promise ring.' Luke gave it to me. It's his promise that someday we'll be married."

Her mother looked dumbstruck and Julie felt a thrill of triumphant satisfaction. "I had no idea the two of you were that serious," Patricia Ellis said slowly.

"Well, we are. And as long as I can be here for Luke, I will be." Julie was amazed that she could have lived so long under the same roof with her mother and still feel so far apart from her. The woman didn't understand, and she never would.

"We need to talk more about this, Julie."

"No we don't. I've made up my mind. I'm not leaving Luke." Julie crossed her arms in stubborn defiance, all but daring her mother to argue with her.

She never got the chance. The phone on Julie's desk rang and when Julie grabbed the receiver, she heard Nancy's anguished voice say, "I just called an ambulance to come get Luke. He's bad off, Julie. Really bad. And I'm scared. Can you meet me at Waterton General right away?"

23

At the hospital, Julie and her mother learned that Luke was having difficulty breathing and that his mother had called the ambulance in a panic. "You did the correct thing," Dr. Portage assured her after he'd examined Luke.

"Will he be all right? Can I take him home?"

"He's still in respiratory distress, so I'm admitting him. I've put him on a respirator."

Nancy cried out and Julie felt wobbly on her feet.

"It's only temporary, simply a way to help him breathe more easily for a spell. I'm ordering X rays to find out why he's in trouble." As an afterthought, Dr. Portage added, "As long as he's on the respirator, he won't be able to talk, so I'll keep him sedated too."

Numb, still shaking from an adrenaline rush of fear, Julie sank slowly into a waiting room chair. Her mother said a few words to Nancy, then headed for the phone, saying, "I'm calling your father." Bud Ellis was at a meeting.

He arrived to join them in less than thirty minutes. "What now?" he asked.

As Luke's situation was explained to him, Julie watched his shoulders sag and heard him mutter, "Poor kid."

The lobby of the hospital had been decorated for Christmas, which was only two weeks away. A feeling of déjà vu slid over Julie: Luke had spent the previous Christmas in the hospital. She remembered the sense of determination they'd all felt about him getting well and the almost childlike naïveté with which they'd faced the future at that time.

"It's not going to go away, is it, Daddy?" she asked. "It's not ever going to leave Luke alone."

"It docs seem relentless." Her father sighed and shook his head. "This makes no sense to me, Julie. Why should a kid like Luke go through this when he's got so much to live for? I've talked to him about it."

His admission surprised Julie—Luke had

never mentioned it to her. "We've talked too, but we never came up with any answers."

"There aren't any. It's just . . . *life*. But going through something like this sure shows what a person's made of, and in my book, no one is made of finer stuff than Luke."

Julie saw a film of tears swimming in her father's eyes, and the sight rattled her. In all the years she'd lived with him, she'd never seen her father cry.

He cleared his throat. "He's like a son to me."

"Don't give up on him yet. He's still got plenty of fight left in him."

And sure enough, by the next day Luke was breathing easier and had been taken off the respirator. He looked very pale, but he gave Julie a smile and a thumbs-up when she came into his room. "We've got to stop meeting like this," he said in a hoarse whisper.

She'd been warned that the breathing tube they'd inserted in his throat would affect his voice. "Let's go back to L.A.," she said, taking hold of his hand.

"If only we could."

They were alone, but Julie didn't know how long the time would last. Nurses breezed in and out of the room regularly and his mother could pop in at any time. An idea had been forming in her mind for days, and suddenly this seemed like the perfect time to present it. She studied the ring on her finger. "Did you mean what you asked me in L.A.?"

"About marrying you?" His gaze also fell on the silver ring. "I meant it." A shadow of doubt crossed his face. "Are you having second thoughts? Do you want to give the ring back?"

"No way." She seized both his hands and pressed them against her breasts. "Why should we wait to get married, Luke? Why, when it's what both of us want?"

"What do you mean?"

"Let's get married now. It doesn't have to be a fancy ceremony . . . and we can do it here in the hospital if we have to. Your mother, my parents, Solena and Frank, Steve and Diedra—if we can get them here quickly. These are the only people who matter in our lives, so they're the only ones we should invite."

She talked rapidly, hardly breaking for a breath, spilling her long-pent-up emotions. "I don't need a fancy dress . . . why, the one I bought for the Christmas dance last year will do nicely. Oh, I know it's not white, but who cares? You and I know we've never messed around. And the hospital is all fixed up for Christmas, so the ceremony could be really festive. Besides, don't you think a Christmas wedding would be fun? Every anniversary we'd have *two* reasons to celebrate.

"We don't have to have a reception or anything, either. Heck, some cheese and crackers is fine with me. Your mom could whip up one of her fancy cheese dips and my mom could do some kind of cake. Not a wedding cake." She made a face. "I've always thought the icing on those things was too sickly sweet. And once you're out of the hospital we could take a little honeymoon to—oh, anyplace—I don't care—"

Luke freed one hand from her embrace and placed his fingertips against her lips to silence her. "Julie, stop."

She stopped, and the silence in the room was deafening.

"I can't marry you now."

She felt a sinking sensation. "Why? I know you love me, and I love you. What else matters?"

His gaze roamed her face as if absorbing it. "I love you all right. And because I love you, I can't make you a bride and a widow in the same month."

"But the doctors are going to fix you up and you'll go home and wait for a donor. You can't give up, Luke. You can't."

He looked at her so tenderly that she almost started crying. "I know why I'm having trouble breathing, Julie."

She couldn't force herself to ask why. Because not knowing served as a protective shield, and so long as she didn't know, she could hold off the finality of what was happening to him.

"I have a tumor in my lung, Julie." He touched his chest. "And the chemo isn't stopping it from growing. They want to cut it out."

"Operate?" She said the word as if it were alien.

"It's located here"—he pressed his palm against the left side of his chest—"very near my heart. It's compressing my heart and taking over my lung. Surgery's my best hope."

"When?" She felt icy cold and stiff, and forming words took great difficulty.

"Day after tomorrow."

Too soon! her mind cried, but her voice said, "But it will make you better, won't it?"

"They think so."

"Will you do it?"

"I talked it over with Mom and my doctors, and it's what I want to do."

She had fears and doubts. She had a host of reasons why he shouldn't, but she saw his steely look of determination and knew he would do what he wanted and that nothing she could say could dissuade him. Not that she was sure she should try. If surgery offered hope and made him more comfortable during his wait for a marrow donor, perhaps it was worth doing. "I'll be here for you," she said.

He smiled. "The first thing I want to see when I get out of recovery is your face." He rested his palm on her cheek. "And when I close my eyes on the operating table, the thing I'll see inside my mind will be your face."

Tears swam in her eyes. "After this operation is over, after you get your strength back, promise me you'll reconsider marrying me right away."

"We'll talk about it after the surgery." He smoothed his thumb across her lips. "Of course, if we do get married soon, your mother will kill us both and the surgery will have been for nothing."

She gave a short laugh. "I don't care what

my mother thinks. I want to be with you, Luke, for the rest of my life."

His gaze caressed her face. "That suits me fine."

The day before Luke's surgery, Steve and Diedra flew into Chicago, rented a car, and drove over to Waterton, lifting Julie's spirits immensely. When they walked into Luke's room, Steve held up his hand and said, "Now don't panic, nephew. We're only here because word got around that you were driving the doctors and your mother nuts. Besides, we were sick of sushi—that's fish you eat *raw,* in case you don't know it—and your mother promised us a good home-cooked meal."

Luke was all smiles. "You came all this way to see me?"

"You and Julie," Diedra said. Julie had seen the expression of shock that crossed Diedra's face when she'd first seen Luke and how she'd quickly suppressed it. Diedra gave him a hug. "We've missed you two."

"Did you bring pictures from your honeymoon?" Julie asked.

"An albumful," Diedra said.

They spent the afternoon looking through the photos and talking, and later, when Julie and Diedra went down to the snack bar for ice cream and Steve stayed behind with Luke, Julie told Diedra that she and Luke might marry as soon as he recovered from his surgery. "Would you stay for the wedding?" she asked.

"Of course we would." Diedra tipped her head thoughtfully. "After you're married, where will you live?"

"With his mother, I guess. She's a lot more sympathetic about me and Luke than mine. And once he's gotten his new bone marrow, he can finish high school. Then, I'm sure some coach will want him to play college ball. Oh, maybe it won't be a big, well-known college, but a smaller one willing to invest in him."

"So he thinks he can still play football?"

"Absolutely. Once his donor marrow starts working, he'll be cured and go on with his life."

"You're a brave girl, Julie. Not every girl your age would take on such a marriage and its possible problems."

Julie shrugged. "I love him." She swirled the spoon through the half-melted remains of her ice cream. "I wish tomorrow was over. His surgery scares me."

"He's young, and that's in his favor. Plus

the doctors wouldn't operate if they didn't think it would help."

They returned to the room, where Luke's mother had joined him and Steve. Luke looked drowsy. "They gave him medication, so he'll sleep soundly tonight," Nancy said. "But we have to leave now."

Luke reached out for Julie. His eyelids looked heavy and his speech was slurred when he said, "The doctor said I could see you in the morning before I go into surgery. Please see me before they put me to sleep?"

"I'll come early."

"I love you."

She bent and kissed him. "I love you too."

24

Julie couldn't sleep that night, and headed for the hospital at six in the morning even though Luke wasn't scheduled to go into the OR until nine. She arrived at his room just as a nurse was giving him pre-op medication to relax him. One arm was hooked to an IV, but he held Julie tightly with his free arm when she bent over his bed. Although he smelled of medicine, he felt warm, and she longed to climb into bed with him and hold him.

"The others will be here soon," Julie said. "Everyone wants to see you before you go into surgery."

"You look beautiful," he said.

She knew how she really looked—dark circles smudged her under-eye area and she hadn't bothered to put on any makeup except for a little lip gloss. "I'll look better when you come down from recovery."

"Julie, I want to tell you some things before they operate."

"What things?"

"I want you to know I'm okay about this and I want you to be okay about it. No matter what the outcome is."

It felt as if a hand had reached into her chest and clutched her heart. "The outcome is that you'll be all right," she said stubbornly.

"I also want you to know I've done a lot of thinking about some of the things we talked about in L.A. You know, about the hereafter and all. I've been reading up on it in all my spare time." He grinned. "Heaven's a real place, Julie—a beautiful place—and if I can't wait for you at the end of an aisle on our wedding day, I'll wait for you in heaven."

"Luke, you're scaring me—"

"Please, let me finish. I don't want to scare you. I only want you to know that either way this surgery turns out, I'll be fine. I—I just want you to be fine."

"I can't think about losing you. Don't make me."

"You're the best part of my life and I will always love you."

Tears had sprung to her eyes. Behind her, she heard others come into the room, and she knew that his mother, her parents, and Steve and Diedra wanted to be with him too. She felt panicked, afraid of letting go of his hand. "I'll see you in a few hours," she said through gritted teeth.

His eyelids drooped from the sedation, but still he held on to her. "If it's possible to send a message from heaven," he whispered, "I'll get one to you."

She choked back a sob and broke her hold, then stepped aside so that the others could surround his bed. Later, in the hallway, when he was wheeled out of his room for the elevator ride down to the surgical floor, he told the orderlies to hold up. They waited while he looked from face to face of the people who loved him, reminding Julie of a man memorizing a map so that he wouldn't get lost in the dark. Finally, he grinned, handed Julie a folded piece of paper, then gave everyone his thumbs-up signal.

Julie watched as he was wheeled away, listened to the clack-clack of the wheels of his bed and the swish of the elevator doors as they closed behind him. Cut off from him, she shuddered.

"Let's go down to the surgical waiting room," her father said, gently taking her arm.

They trooped down to the area where family and friends waited for news from various operating rooms. A telephone linking the surgical floor with the waiting room would occasionally ring and tell people that their loved one had been taken to recovery and the surgeon would be down to talk to them soon. In the waiting room, Solena and Frank were already camped out on sofas. Julie tried to join them, but found it impossible to sit still.

As the hours dragged by, the phone rang several times, always for others. Every time it rang, Julie jumped. She felt taut and edgy. Around one o'clock, her father tried to get her to eat something, but she refused. She stared down at the floor, listening to the thump of her heart, the whispers of those around her.

Suddenly the waiting room door opened and she looked up to see Luke's surgeon standing in front of their group. Surprised, she glanced at the phone, wondering why she hadn't heard it ring. The doctor removed his green head covering. Julie allowed her eyes to travel the length of him and saw flecks of blood on the green paper coverings of his shoes. *Luke's blood,* she knew instinctively.

"The tumor was far more entrenched than we ever imagined," the surgeon began. "It was totally ingrown to the side of his heart."

Julie heard Nancy begin to sob.

"I'm sorry," the doctor said. "We did everything we could."

Somehow, through it all, Julie didn't lose her composure. She heard questions and answers, but the words didn't make sense. She was beyond caring what was said anyway. Slowly, she stood and removed the folded piece of paper Luke had given her only hours before. She'd deliberately not opened it, saving it for this time when she knew she would need contact with him most.

"What's in the note?" she heard a tearful Solena ask.

Numbly, Julie unfolded the paper. On it, Luke had drawn a single, perfect flower.

The day of Luke's funeral, snow blanketed the ground. Cold white drifts covered cars and fences and the sky was a dull shade of leaden gray. To Julie, riding in the funeral home's limo to the cemetery, the whole world looked black and white. Void of color.

The high school closed for the day and almost the whole city turned out to bury their hometown hero. On Main Street, traffic lights blinked yellow and a police escort led the long, lonely precession to Luke's final resting place. Julie wore black, including a black mantilla over her long blond hair. She sat in the car sandwiched between Nancy and Steve. In the limo's other long seat were Diedra and her parents. The trip seemed slow, endless.

"I never thought I'd have to do this again," Nancy said tonelessly, and Julie knew she was remembering her husband's funeral so many years before. Luke's mother stared through the window. "Who will ride with me when it's my turn?"

No one answered, and Julie tightened her hold on the edge of the car seat. Inside, she felt as dead as the world outside the car window seemed. As empty as the stretches of snow between the headstones of the cemetery.

At the burial site, hundreds had gathered, all dressed in shades of black and gray. The car stopped, and attendants helped Julie and the others make the walk to the tarpaulin-covered pit where Luke's casket would be placed. Because the ground was frozen, a special machine had been used to dig the hole. Julie could still see its tracks in the packed snow. She heard the crunch of snow beneath her boots, felt the sting of frigid air on her face.

Julie watched as Frank led the pallbearers— all members of the football team and wearing black armbands—toward them. A mantle of flowers, each one as white as the snow, cascaded down the sides of the steel-gray casket. The petals of the flowers were frozen, singed by ice, brittle and stiff. Unbidden, Luke's long-ago words came to her. *"Someday, I'll dress you in flowers,"* he had said. Instead, it was he who had been wrapped in blossoms.

She hardly heard the brief ceremony. She felt isolated and cut off from reality, not caring what was said. No words could make a difference. Luke was gone and nothing could bring him back. Her movements were mechanical, like an elaborate puppet's. She went through the motions, but in her heart, she was hollow and empty. And cold. So very cold.

Once the ceremony was over, Julie's parents urged Nancy to receive friends at their home because it was so much more spacious. People arrived steadily all day, bringing food and flowers and small gifts. Nancy, ever gracious and kind, accepted every expression of grief over the loss of her son. But Julie felt removed from the ritual, abhorring it. Still, she knew it meant a great deal to Luke's mother, so she tolerated it.

Late in the afternoon, as it grew dark and colder, Diedra found Julie in the backyard, huddled against a leafless and barren oak tree. "Steve and I are leaving for the airport," she said gently. "We have to go home to L.A."

"Good-bye," Julie told her. How far away and long ago L.A. seemed.

"You should come in the house, Julie. It's cold and you'll get sick."

"So what?"

Diedra smoothed Julie's hair, flecked with snow from the blackened branches of the tree. "Please come visit us this summer. Will you promise me you'll come?"

Julie traced her fingers along the roughened bark of the old tree trunk. "See our initials? Luke carved them for us when he was twelve." The letters looked scarred and shrunken by the cold. She brushed them lightly with gloved fingers.

"You're breaking my heart, Julie. Please tell me you're going to be all right."

"Luke used to bring me flowers."

Steve called to Diedra from the porch.

"I've got to go, honey." She hugged Julie,

who stood motionless. "Don't forget—we're expecting to see you this summer."

Julie didn't answer; she only brushed her fingertips over the worn initials as Diedra left.

Later, when her house had emptied and her father was taking Nancy home, Julie wearily climbed the stairs to her room. She stripped, dropping her clothes in a heap onto her floor, pulled on a flannel nightshirt, and climbed into her bed.

After knocking lightly, her mother opened the door and entered the room. The light flooding in from the hallway blinded Julie, and she turned away from its glare. "Julie . . ." Her mother halted beside her bed. "Honey . . . if there's anything you want . . ."

"I want Luke," she said without emotion.

"Honey . . . please . . . I'm sorry . . . so sorry . . ."

"Good night," Julie said, then curled into a tight ball and pulled the covers over her head. Minutes later, she heard her mother leave the room. "Luke," she whispered into the darkness. "Why have you left me all alone?"

25

"Julie, your mother and I are very concerned about you." Bud Ellis sat on the side of Julie's bed, looking helpless, his big hands folded in his lap.

"I'm fine, Dad."

"You're *not* fine," Julie's mother interjected. "You don't eat, you don't go to school, you don't see your friends. Julie, you've lain in that bed for over a month. You've lost so much weight we hardly recognize you. Please, honey, snap out of it."

Julie peered dully up at her parents. Why didn't they leave her alone? Food had lost its taste and appeal. And she'd tried to go back to school after Luke's funeral, but she couldn't concentrate and she couldn't keep up in her classes. All she wanted to do was sleep. Because when she was asleep, she could forget how much she hurt. "I'll try to get up later," she said in an effort to placate her parents. "Right now, I'm too tired."

She saw her father glance up at her mother. He sighed and touched her shoulder through her bedcovers. "I miss him too, Julie. Every day, I think about him. But what you're doing to yourself isn't right. You can't curl up and die too."

Curl up and die. The idea didn't sound so bad to her. Without Luke, she certainly couldn't think about *living*.

"Why don't you get up, get dressed, and come into school with me," her father said.

"I'll make you late." Her bedside clock read eight-thirty. Usually, he was gone by seven-thirty.

"Who cares? I'm the coach, remember? Besides, first period is my free period this semester. Come on—drive in with me."

"Not today. You and Mom go on without me. I'll rest and maybe when you get home this afternoon, I'll feel better."

Her father rose, but her mother kicked off her shoes. "If you're staying home again, I will too."

Julie was mildly surprised. Her mother rarely missed work, and now that second semester had begun, more and more kids would be seeking her services at the high school for help with college applications. "You don't have to stay home. I'm just going to stay in bed today." Her thoughts grew fuzzy.

Julie heard her parents whispering at her door. Then her father left and her mother came back to her bedside. "Solena called last night. She wants to come over after school."

"I don't think I'm up to visitors. Tell her I'll call her later."

"Julie, you've been putting her off for days. She's your best friend and she calls every day asking about you."

Julie felt tears brim in her eyes. All this conversation was confusing her, upsetting her. She sniffed and turned over to face the wall. "Please, not today. I—I just don't want to have to see anybody today."

Minutes later, she heard her mother softly close the bedroom door, and soon afterward, Julie fell into the welcoming arms of a deep, dark, dreamless sleep.

Afternoon sunlight streamed through Julie's bedroom window, awakening her. Someone had pulled up her window shade, and the winter sun cut a path across her bed and pillow.

She buried her face under her covers, but the light was relentless. Who had done such a thing? she wondered.

She sighed and realized that the only way to shut out the sun was to get up and pull down the shade, but her arms and legs felt almost too heavy with exhaustion to move. She forced herself upright, staggered to the window, leaned over her desk, and fumbled at the cord for the shade.

From the kitchen below she heard her mother moving around and smelled the aroma of simmering chicken soup. Normally, the aroma would make her mouth water, but today it made her feel nauseous. She yanked down the shade and returned to her bed, then buried herself under the covers until she heard her mother come into her room.

"How about supper in bed?" her mother asked cheerfully, setting down a tray laden with soup, crackers, milk, and green Jell-O. When Julie was a small child, green gelatin had been her favorite.

"I'm not hungry."

Her mother sat on the bed and pulled Julie's covers from off her head. "Look at me, Julie."

Julie struggled to focus.

"This has got to stop. Your father and I can't bear to see you wasting away like this."

"Please, Mom, don't—"

"No. You listen! I've talked with our doctor, and he says that the way you've been grieving is cause for alarm. When I told him how much weight you've lost, he said it might be necessary not only to get you counseling, but to hospitalize you and put you on an IV."

Julie wanted to be angry, but she didn't have the energy for it.

"So sit up and eat or I will drive you to the hospital personally and check you in."

Wearily, Julie obeyed. "I'm up, but I still don't want to eat."

"You have a visitor," her mother announced without preamble.

"Tell Solena to come back tomorrow."

"It isn't Solena."

The bedroom door inched open, and Nancy peeked into the room. "Hi, Julie. Can I come in?"

Julie hadn't seen her since the funeral, and seeing her now caused fresh pain to stab at her heart. Still, although Nancy looked tired and she'd lost weight, she also looked serene. "Sure. Come in."

Pat Ellis moved so that Nancy could take her place on the bed. "Your mother tells me you're not doing so good."

Feeling betrayed, Julie glared at her mother. "I'm tired, that's all."

"You're depressed," Nancy corrected. "I've been depressed too, but not like you." She placed her hands on Julie's. "I lost my only son, Julie. I'll never get over the pain. But I will get on with my life."

"What do you mean?"

"I'm moving out to L.A. Steve's offered me a job. He and Diedra are starting a small production company and they need an office manager. Luke talked to him before the surgery and asked Steve to take care of me." A wistful smile turned up the corners of her mouth. "Just like Luke—to be worried about me. Anyway, I'm going where there are no memories to haunt me every day."

The news jolted Julie. Her last link with Luke was being broken. "When will you go?"

"Just as soon as my house sells."

Tears filled Julie's eyes. "I'll miss you."

"We've been through a lot together through the years. Frankly, I've grown to love you like a daughter. That's why it hurts me to see you harming yourself this way."

Julie dropped her gaze, unable to speak around the lump in her throat.

"Luke wouldn't have wanted you to do this to yourself, you know. He wanted the best for you. He wanted you to be happy."

"How can I be happy without him?"

"I don't know . . . all I know is that someday, you will be. You'll be happy"—she paused—"and you'll fall in love again."

Julie shook her head adamantly. "I'll never love anybody the way I loved Luke. I won't risk being hurt again."

"Love is always a risk. Just like Luke's surgery." Nancy smoothed Julie's tangled hair. "Just before he went back to the hospital, the bone marrow donor program had found him a match."

Julie gasped. "They did? Why didn't he tell me? Why didn't he get the transplant?"

"Because even if the transplant had worked, the tumor wasn't going away. He made the decision to risk the surgery and do the transplant afterward."

"Are you saying that he knew he might not live through the operation from the start?"

"Yes."

"But why?" The information tortured her.

"Because in his mind, the benefit out-weighed the risks. With the tumor gone, the bone marrow transplant had a better chance of working."

"But if he'd had the transplant first, maybe he'd still be alive. He took the risk for nothing."

Nancy shook her head. "He told me that life is full of risks and that if a person doesn't take them, life is very shallow. And he said to me, 'Mom, dead is dead.' Luke hated dying by degrees. He told me that he'd rather have dying over with all at once than have it happen bit by bit."

Julie felt no consolation. "What am I going to do without him?"

"You're going to live your life. You're going to honor him by doing the things you would have done if he'd never gotten sick and died."

"How can I?"

"The same as all of us—one day at a time." Nancy put her arms around Julie and held her for a long time. Finally, she pulled away, saying, "I'll let you know when my house sells. Please come see me before I move. And once I settle in L.A., I want you to visit me there. Please take care of yourself, Julie."

When she was gone, Julie flopped wearily back against her pillow, going over the meaning of Nancy's words in her mind. *Luke had known he would probably die, but he had the surgery anyway.* She saw his face, his thumbs-up, his broad, sunny smile as he disappeared behind the OR doors.

Her mother stepped forward, holding the food tray. She set it on Julie's lap and picked up the bowl of soup, stirring it, until the aroma and warmth filled the air. "Listen to Nancy, Julie. She knows what she's saying. Life is for the living."

Julie felt an unbearable weight of sadness press against her chest, but her mother looked so expectant, Julie reached for the soup spoon.

"No," her mother said softly. "Please, let me help you."

Their gazes locked, and Julie saw a tenderness in the depths of her mother's eyes that shook her. "All right," Julie whispered.

Then her mother smiled, ladled soup into the spoon, and held it to Julie's lips, feeding her slowly and expertly, as she hadn't done since Julie was a tiny child.

It took Julie another three weeks to regain her strength and begin putting on lost pounds.

She also began studying at home, attempting assignments, doing take-home tests. She began to talk to her friends again and decided to return to school the first of April.

Her return was bittersweet. Luke's presence haunted the halls, and sometimes she could swear she saw his baseball cap bobbing through the crowds as they moved between classes. But kids were genuinely glad to see her, stopping her, talking to her, sharing memories of Luke with her. Her mother helped her tremendously with makeup work and arranged special tutoring for the classes Julie was too far behind in to catch up with on her own. She structured a summer tutorial program, so that even though Julie wouldn't technically graduate with her class in June, she would at least be able to receive her diploma at the end of the summer.

One Saturday, Julie was reading on the back deck in a patch of sunlight, a blanket thrown over her lap, when her father rushed out the door. "Honey, quick! Come with me!"

Startled, she gawked at him. His eyes were glowing, his expression excited. "What's happening?"

"I can't tell you. I have to show you. Come on."

"Dad, I really don't want—"

He tugged her to her feet. "You have to come with me to the football stadium and see this with your own eyes. You're not going to believe it, Julie. But you have to see it."

26

Julie hadn't thought about the new football stadium in many months. And she didn't want to see it now, but her father was so excited, she couldn't refuse him. At the stadium, he screeched to a halt, leaped from the car, and hurried to open her door. "You need to get up high," he said, taking her hand. "Then you can see it better."

Julie climbed the cement bleachers obediently, forcing herself not to think about all the times she'd come to the stadium with Luke.

When they were about a third of the way up, Julie had to stop and catch her breath. "Sorry," she told her father. "I'm out of shape."

"No problem. This is high enough anyway. Look." He pointed down toward the field.

She turned and let her gaze follow his finger. A fine stubble of wild grass blanketed the rough, rutted field with green fuzz. But there was something else sprouting in the center of the field. Green stems, arranged in neat rows, were emerging from the caked earth. She squinted. "What's growing?"

"Tulips."

"Why would you plant tulips in the middle of your football field? You told me it had to be smoothed out and sodded."

"I didn't plant them."

Slowly, the truth dawned on her. "Luke?"

"I'm sure of it," her father said. "It'll take a couple of weeks until they're all up and blooming, but once they're finished, I think you'll see a pattern of some kind. Like a design he planned out."

She remembered Luke's words: *"If it's possible to send a message from heaven, I'll get one to you."* Tears blurred her eyes. "But how? When?"

"Tulips have to be planted by October, or November at the latest, before the ground freezes, so I figure that's when he must have done it."

"Right after he went back on chemo."

"Probably so."

She clapped her hand across her mouth to

stifle a sob. Her father pulled her into his arms. "Julie-girl, it's all right. Go ahead and cry. He meant this for you, honey. He did this even though he knew he might not be here to share it with you."

She imagined Luke arriving in the dark of night, digging holes in the hard ground, dropping each bulb into each hole, and covering it over so that no one could tell what he'd done. The bulbs had lain dormant beneath the snow all winter long until the gentle fingers of spring had awakened them. Like the thawing snow, she felt her grief begin to soften, her terrible pain begin to melt.

Every day afterward, Julie returned to the stadium, climbed the steps, and watched Luke's testimony of tulips bloom in a rainbow of spring colors—red, yellow, purple, hot pink. The stems stood tall and straight, one series arranged in a single line, another in a crudely shaped heart, the final one in the shape of the letter U. *I love you.* Just as Luke had carved on the oak tree in her backyard the summer before.

Late one afternoon, while she waited for her father down on the field, a bulldozer roared to life and rolled through double gates at one of the end zones. "No!" Julie cried, bolting toward the big yellow machine.

Suddenly, her father emerged from one of the stadium tunnels and parked his large body squarely in front of the dozer. "What do you think you're doing?" he yelled up at the driver.

"Got a work order, buddy," the driver shouted over the noise of the engine. "I need to level the field so the sod trucks can come in and get it planted tomorrow."

"Daddy, don't let him," Julie begged.

"Not yet," Bud Ellis told the dozer driver. "It's not ready to be leveled yet."

"But this work order—"

"I'm the football coach at this school, and I'll take responsibility for changing your order."

The driver looked doubtful. "I don't know . . ."

"Not today," Julie said boldly.

"Okay. So when?"

"When the tulips finish blooming."

"What?" The driver looked at her as if she were insane.

"You heard the lady," Bud Ellis said. "When the tulips are gone."

She left them arguing about it and walked out onto the field, where she knelt next to a row of colorful flowers and gently fingered the waxy petals.

In her mind's eye, she saw Luke's face, his playful grin, and she smiled back at him.

"So, you're still sending me flowers," she said to his image. "Do you think you can fix *everything* with flowers?"

In the hazy sunlight, his image nodded, gave her a thumbs-up, and faded away into the spring air.

Julie blinked, glanced around, and realized that she was standing by herself in the middle of a football field blooming with tulips. Luke was gone. But he was waiting for her somewhere. Somewhere, on the other side of all her tomorrows.

Look for Lurlene McDaniel's next book, *I'll Be Seeing You:*

When a chemistry experiment explodes, seventeen-year-old Kyle is left blinded and deeply depressed. As he is recovering in the hospital, he is befriended by Carley, a patient in the room next door. Carley becomes Kyle's eyes and his cheerleader, giving him hope and a link to the outside world.

Carley has never met a boy as handsome as Kyle. She knows that boys like girls who are pretty—and she is not. Scarred by a facial deformity that no plastic surgeon can fix, she has, over the years, used her sense of humor to cope. But now that she's become so close to Kyle, she's worried that once his bandages are removed—*if* they are removed—and he sees her, it will be the end of their relationship. Carley wants the best for Kyle, yet what will it mean for her?

FREE LIBRARY